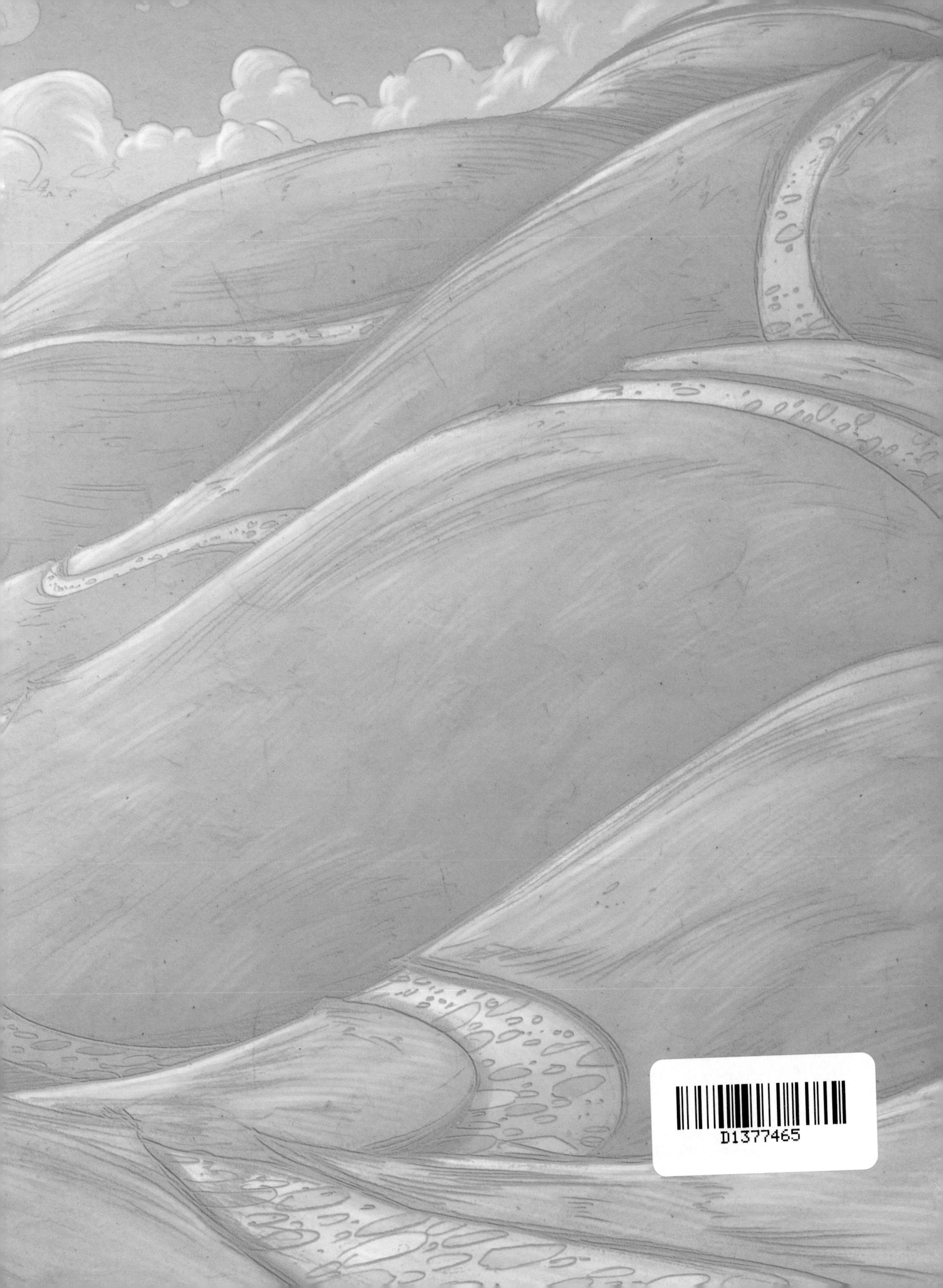

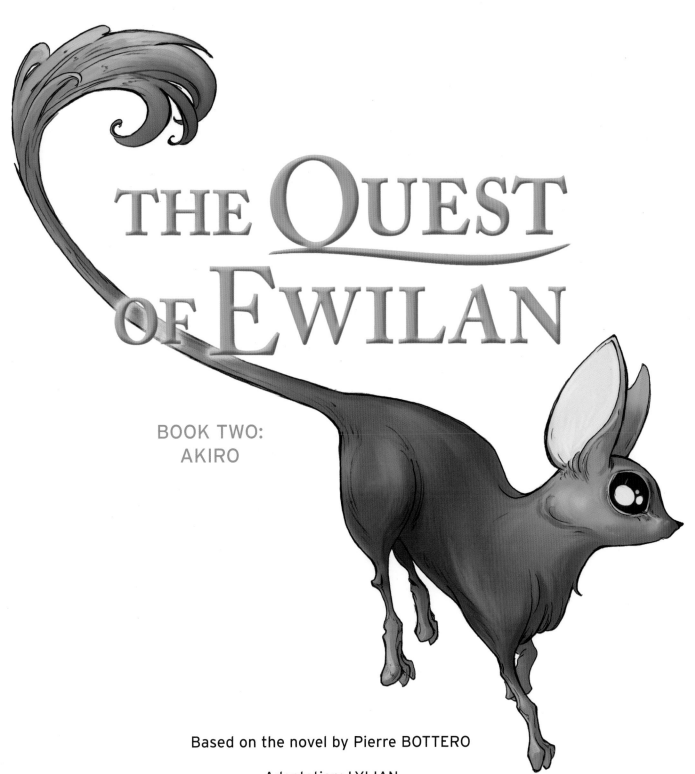

THE QUEST OF EWILAN

BOOK TWO: AKIRO

Based on the novel by Pierre BOTTERO

Adaptation: LYLIAN
Art: Laurence BALDETTI
Coloring: Loïc CHEVALLIER

EURO COMICS
ENGLISH EDITION   GRAPHIC NOVELS

An imprint of IDW PUBLISHING

EDITED BY **Dean Mullaney**
ART DIRECTOR **Lorraine Turner**
TRANSLATION **Edward Gauvin**

EuroComics.us

EuroComics is an imprint of
IDW Publishing
a Division of Idea and Design Works, LLC
2765 Truxtun Road • San Diego, CA 92106
www.idwpublishing.com

Distributed to the book trade by Penguin Random House
Distributed to the comic book trade by Diamond Book Distributors

ISBN: 978-1-68405-543-2
First Printing, August 2019

IDW Publishing
Chris Ryall, President, Publisher, & CCO
John Barber, Editor-in-Chief
Cara Morrison, Chief Financial Officer
Matt Ruzicka, Chief Accounting Officer
David Hedgecock, Associate Publisher
Jerry Bennington, VP of New Product Development
Lorelei Bunjes, VP of Digital Services
Justin Eisinger, Editorial Director, Graphic Novels & Collections
Eric Moss, Senior Director, Licensing and Business Development

Ted Adams and Robbie Robbins, IDW Founders
THANKS TO:
Ivanka Hahnenberger, Justin Eisinger, and Alonzo Simon.

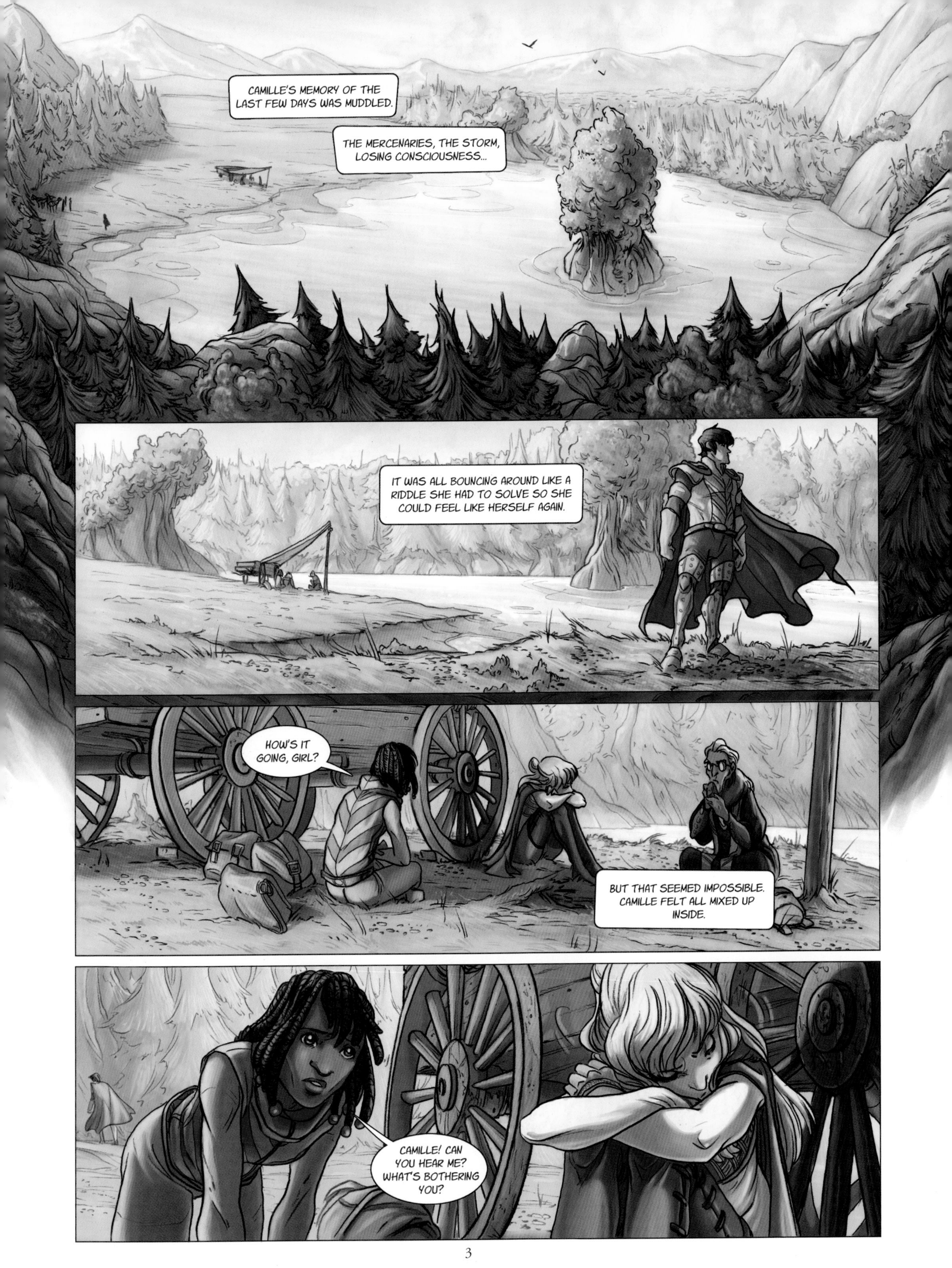
CAMILLE'S MEMORY OF THE LAST FEW DAYS WAS MUDDLED.
THE MERCENARIES, THE STORM, LOSING CONSCIOUSNESS...
IT WAS ALL BOUNCING AROUND LIKE A RIDDLE SHE HAD TO SOLVE SO SHE COULD FEEL LIKE HERSELF AGAIN.
HOW'S IT GOING, GIRL?
BUT THAT SEEMED IMPOSSIBLE. CAMILLE FELT ALL MIXED UP INSIDE.
CAMILLE! CAN YOU HEAR ME? WHAT'S BOTHERING YOU?

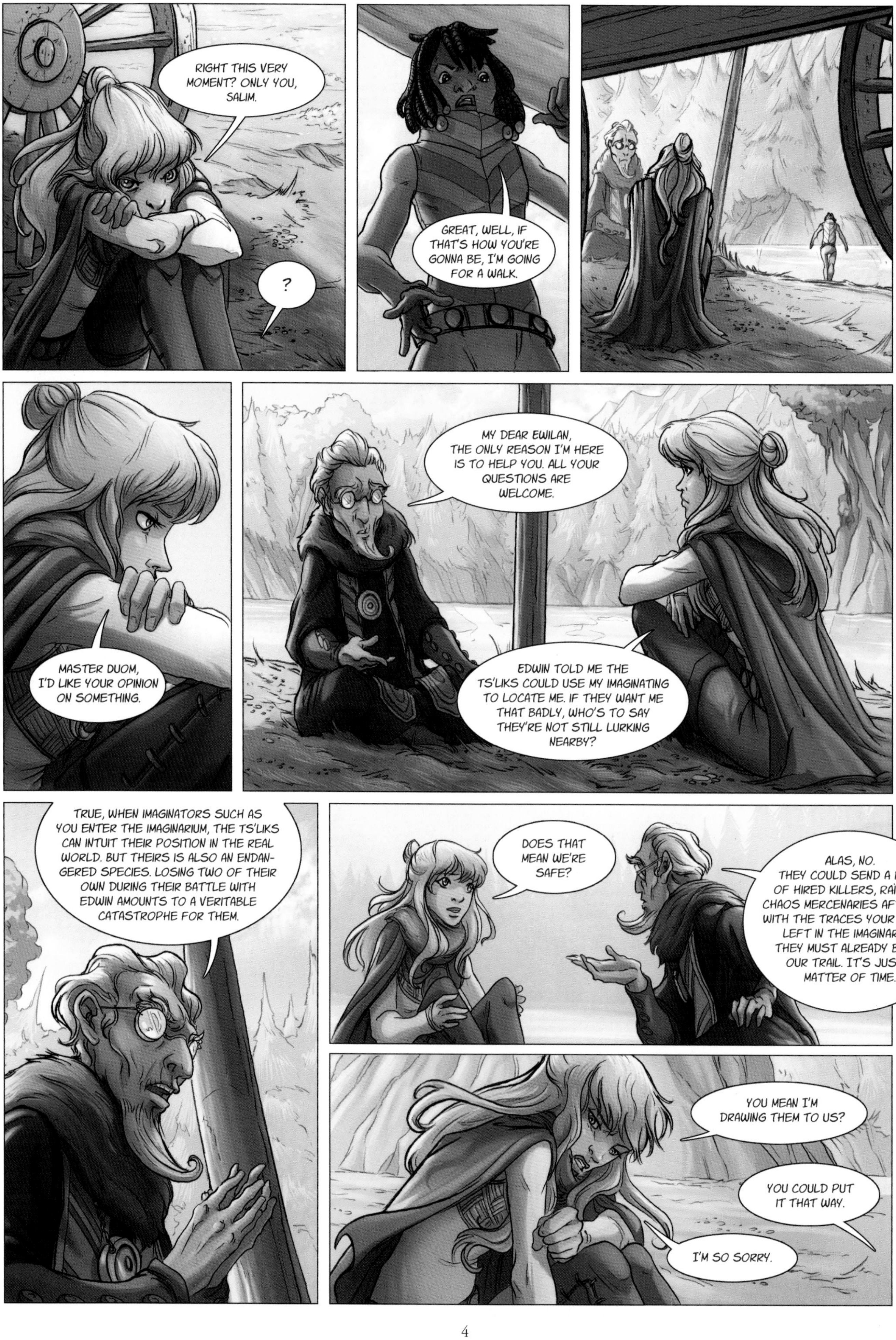
RIGHT THIS VERY MOMENT? ONLY YOU, SALIM.
?
GREAT, WELL, IF THAT'S HOW YOU'RE GONNA BE, I'M GOING FOR A WALK.
MASTER DUOM, I'D LIKE YOUR OPINION ON SOMETHING.
MY DEAR EWILAN, THE ONLY REASON I'M HERE IS TO HELP YOU. ALL YOUR QUESTIONS ARE WELCOME.
EDWIN TOLD ME THE TS'LIKS COULD USE MY IMAGINATING TO LOCATE ME. IF THEY WANT ME THAT BADLY, WHO'S TO SAY THEY'RE NOT STILL LURKING NEARBY?
TRUE, WHEN IMAGINATORS SUCH AS YOU ENTER THE IMAGINARIUM, THE TS'LIKS CAN INTUIT THEIR POSITION IN THE REAL WORLD. BUT THEIRS IS ALSO AN ENDAN-GERED SPECIES. LOSING TWO OF THEIR OWN DURING THEIR BATTLE WITH EDWIN AMOUNTS TO A VERITABLE CATASTROPHE FOR THEM.
DOES THAT MEAN WE'RE SAFE?
ALAS, NO. THEY COULD SEND A PACK OF HIRED KILLERS, RAÏS, OR CHAOS MERCENARIES AFTER US. WITH THE TRACES YOUR STORM LEFT IN THE IMAGINARIUM, THEY MUST ALREADY BE ON OUR TRAIL. IT'S JUST A MATTER OF TIME.
YOU MEAN I'M DRAWING THEM TO US?
YOU COULD PUT IT THAT WAY.
I'M SO SORRY.

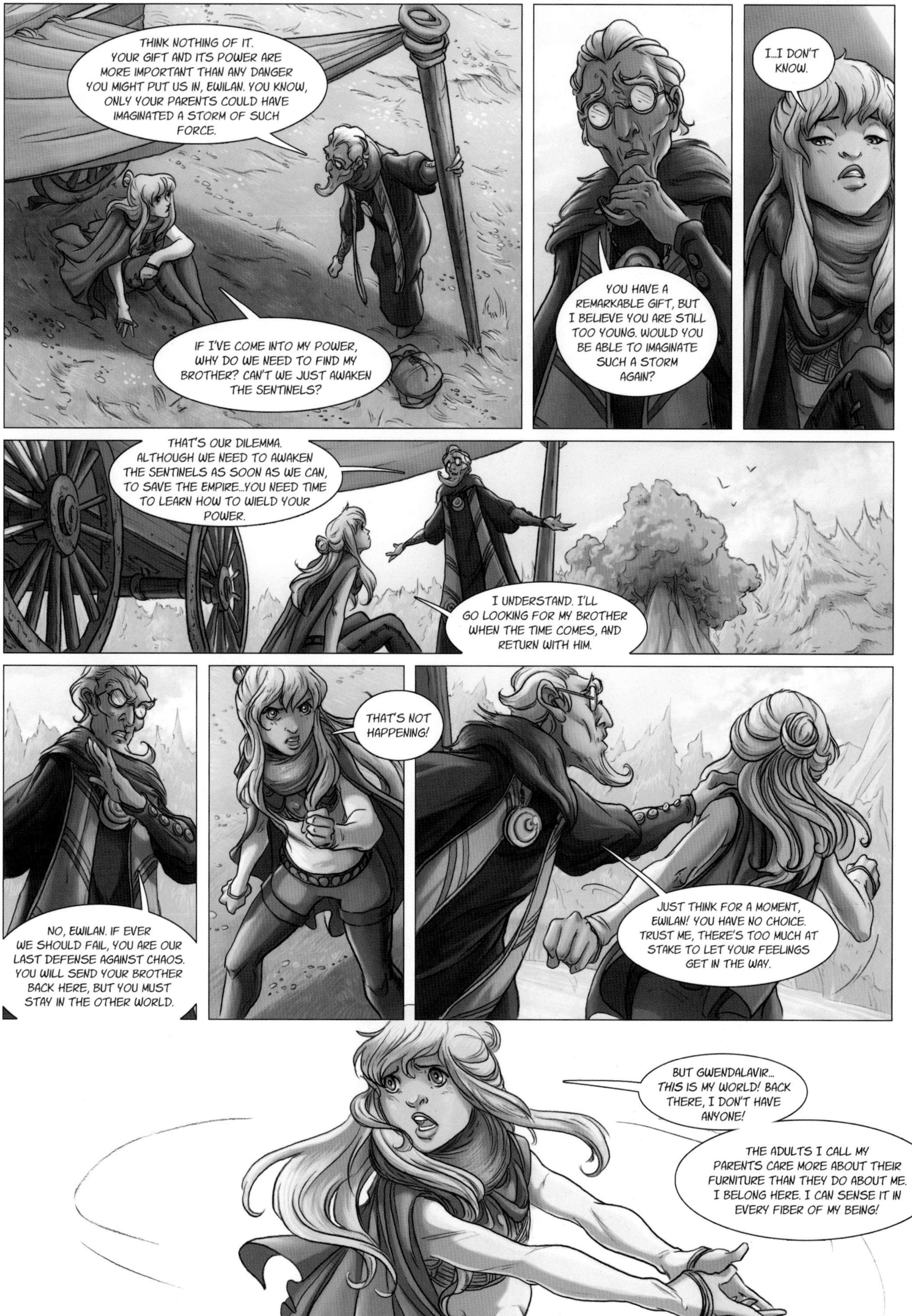
THINK NOTHING OF IT. YOUR GIFT AND ITS POWER ARE MORE IMPORTANT THAN ANY DANGER YOU MIGHT PUT US IN, EWILAN. YOU KNOW, ONLY YOUR PARENTS COULD HAVE IMAGINATED A STORM OF SUCH FORCE.
IF I'VE COME INTO MY POWER, WHY DO WE NEED TO FIND MY BROTHER? CAN'T WE JUST AWAKEN THE SENTINELS?
YOU HAVE A REMARKABLE GIFT, BUT I BELIEVE YOU ARE STILL TOO YOUNG. WOULD YOU BE ABLE TO IMAGINATE SUCH A STORM AGAIN?
I...I DON'T KNOW.
THAT'S OUR DILEMMA. ALTHOUGH WE NEED TO AWAKEN THE SENTINELS AS SOON AS WE CAN, TO SAVE THE EMPIRE...YOU NEED TIME TO LEARN HOW TO WIELD YOUR POWER.
I UNDERSTAND. I'LL GO LOOKING FOR MY BROTHER WHEN THE TIME COMES, AND RETURN WITH HIM.
NO, EWILAN. IF EVER WE SHOULD FAIL, YOU ARE OUR LAST DEFENSE AGAINST CHAOS. YOU WILL SEND YOUR BROTHER BACK HERE, BUT YOU MUST STAY IN THE OTHER WORLD.
THAT'S NOT HAPPENING!
JUST THINK FOR A MOMENT, EWILAN! YOU HAVE NO CHOICE. TRUST ME, THERE'S TOO MUCH AT STAKE TO LET YOUR FEELINGS GET IN THE WAY.
BUT GWENDALAVIR... THIS IS MY WORLD! BACK THERE, I DON'T HAVE ANYONE!
THE ADULTS I CALL MY PARENTS CARE MORE ABOUT THEIR FURNITURE THAN THEY DO ABOUT ME. I BELONG HERE. I CAN SENSE IT IN EVERY FIBER OF MY BEING!

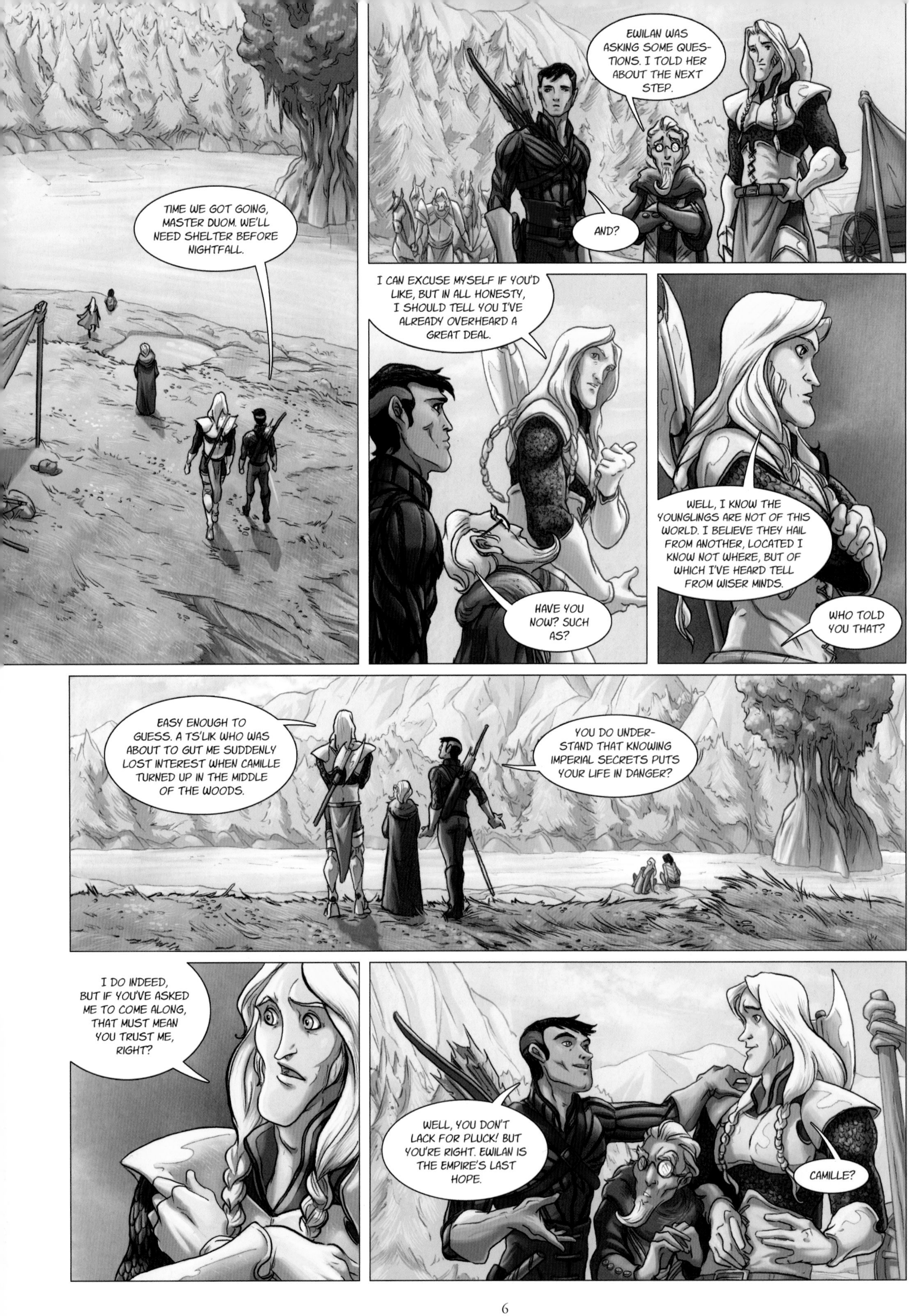
TIME WE GOT GOING, MASTER DUOM. WE'LL NEED SHELTER BEFORE NIGHTFALL.
EWILAN WAS ASKING SOME QUES-TIONS. I TOLD HER ABOUT THE NEXT STEP.
AND?
I CAN EXCUSE MYSELF IF YOU'D LIKE, BUT IN ALL HONESTY, I SHOULD TELL YOU I'VE ALREADY OVERHEARD A GREAT DEAL.
HAVE YOU NOW? SUCH AS?
WELL, I KNOW THE YOUNGLINGS ARE NOT OF THIS WORLD. I BELIEVE THEY HAIL FROM ANOTHER, LOCATED I KNOW NOT WHERE, BUT OF WHICH I'VE HEARD TELL FROM WISER MINDS.
WHO TOLD YOU THAT?
EASY ENOUGH TO GUESS. A TS'LIK WHO WAS ABOUT TO GUT ME SUDDENLY LOST INTEREST WHEN CAMILLE TURNED UP IN THE MIDDLE OF THE WOODS.
YOU DO UNDER-STAND THAT KNOWING IMPERIAL SECRETS PUTS YOUR LIFE IN DANGER?
I DO INDEED, BUT IF YOU'VE ASKED ME TO COME ALONG, THAT MUST MEAN YOU TRUST ME, RIGHT?
WELL, YOU DON'T LACK FOR PLUCK! BUT YOU'RE RIGHT. EWILAN IS THE EMPIRE'S LAST HOPE.
CAMILLE?

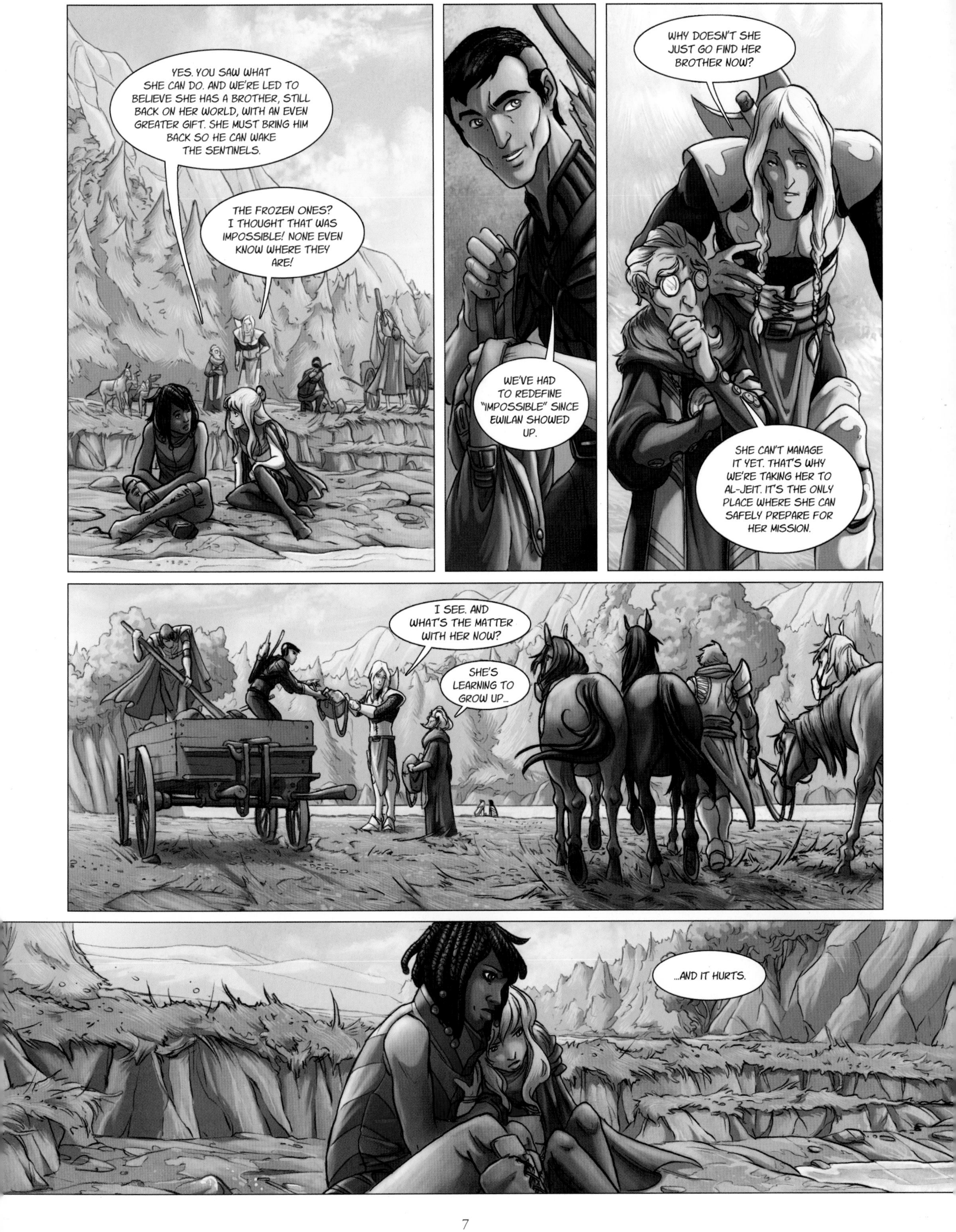
YES. YOU SAW WHAT SHE CAN DO. AND WE'RE LED TO BELIEVE SHE HAS A BROTHER, STILL BACK ON HER WORLD, WITH AN EVEN GREATER GIFT. SHE MUST BRING HIM BACK SO HE CAN WAKE THE SENTINELS.
THE FROZEN ONES? I THOUGHT THAT WAS IMPOSSIBLE! NONE EVEN KNOW WHERE THEY ARE!
WE'VE HAD TO REDEFINE "IMPOSSIBLE" SINCE EWILAN SHOWED UP.
WHY DOESN'T SHE JUST GO FIND HER BROTHER NOW?
SHE CAN'T MANAGE IT YET. THAT'S WHY WE'RE TAKING HER TO AL-JEIT. IT'S THE ONLY PLACE WHERE SHE CAN SAFELY PREPARE FOR HER MISSION.
I SEE. AND WHAT'S THE MATTER WITH HER NOW?
SHE'S LEARNING TO GROW UP...
...AND IT HURTS.

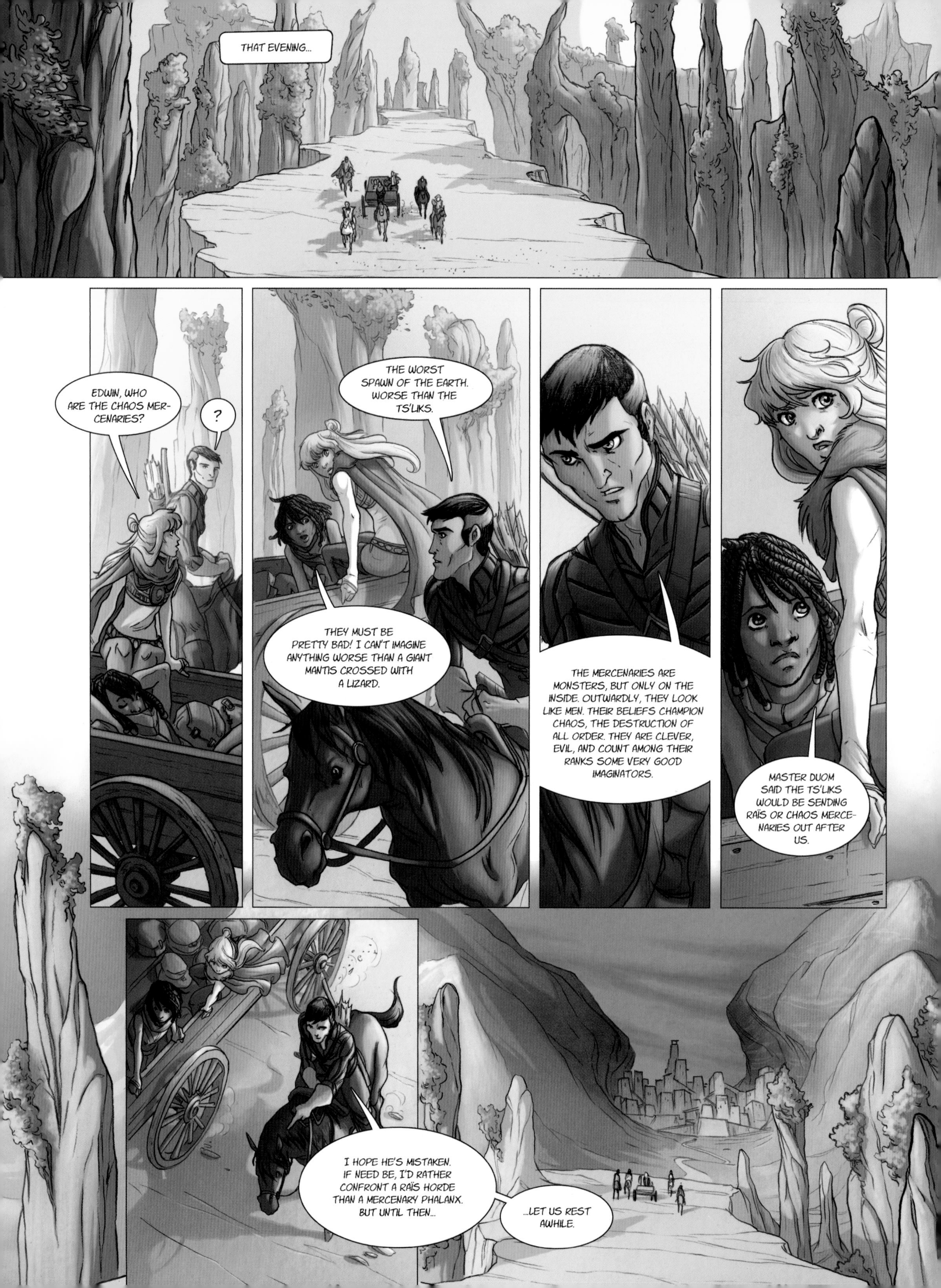
THAT EVENING...
EDWIN, WHO ARE THE CHAOS MERCENARIES?
?
THE WORST SPAWN OF THE EARTH. WORSE THAN THE TS'LIKS.
THEY MUST BE PRETTY BAD! I CAN'T IMAGINE ANYTHING WORSE THAN A GIANT MANTIS CROSSED WITH A LIZARD.
THE MERCENARIES ARE MONSTERS, BUT ONLY ON THE INSIDE. OUTWARDLY, THEY LOOK LIKE MEN. THEIR BELIEFS CHAMPION CHAOS, THE DESTRUCTION OF ALL ORDER. THEY ARE CLEVER, EVIL, AND COUNT AMONG THEIR RANKS SOME VERY GOOD IMAGINATORS.
MASTER DUOM SAID THE TS'LIKS WOULD BE SENDING RAÏS OR CHAOS MERCENARIES OUT AFTER US.
I HOPE HE'S MISTAKEN. IF NEED BE, I'D RATHER CONFRONT A RAÏS HORDE THAN A MERCENARY PHALANX. BUT UNTIL THEN...
...LET US REST AWHILE.

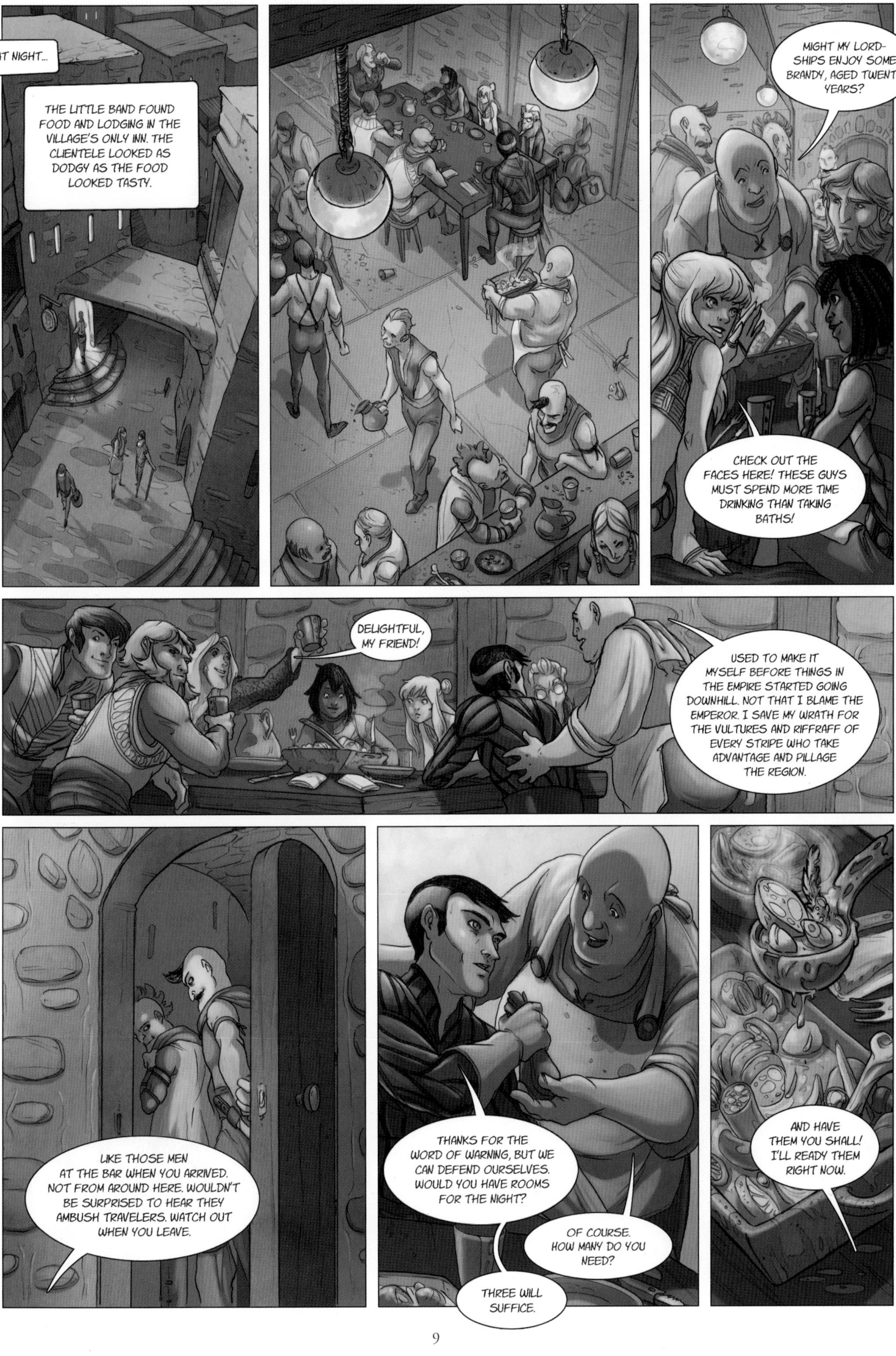

THAT NIGHT...
THE LITTLE BAND FOUND FOOD AND LODGING IN THE VILLAGE'S ONLY INN. THE CLIENTELE LOOKED AS DODGY AS THE FOOD LOOKED TASTY.
MIGHT MY LORD-SHIPS ENJOY SOME BRANDY, AGED TWENTY YEARS?
CHECK OUT THE FACES HERE! THESE GUYS MUST SPEND MORE TIME DRINKING THAN TAKING BATHS!
DELIGHTFUL, MY FRIEND!
USED TO MAKE IT MYSELF BEFORE THINGS IN THE EMPIRE STARTED GOING DOWNHILL. NOT THAT I BLAME THE EMPEROR. I SAVE MY WRATH FOR THE VULTURES AND RIFFRAFF OF EVERY STRIPE WHO TAKE ADVANTAGE AND PILLAGE THE REGION.
LIKE THOSE MEN AT THE BAR WHEN YOU ARRIVED. NOT FROM AROUND HERE. WOULDN'T BE SURPRISED TO HEAR THEY AMBUSH TRAVELERS. WATCH OUT WHEN YOU LEAVE.
THANKS FOR THE WORD OF WARNING, BUT WE CAN DEFEND OURSELVES. WOULD YOU HAVE ROOMS FOR THE NIGHT?
OF COURSE. HOW MANY DO YOU NEED?
THREE WILL SUFFICE.
AND HAVE THEM YOU SHALL! I'LL READY THEM RIGHT NOW.

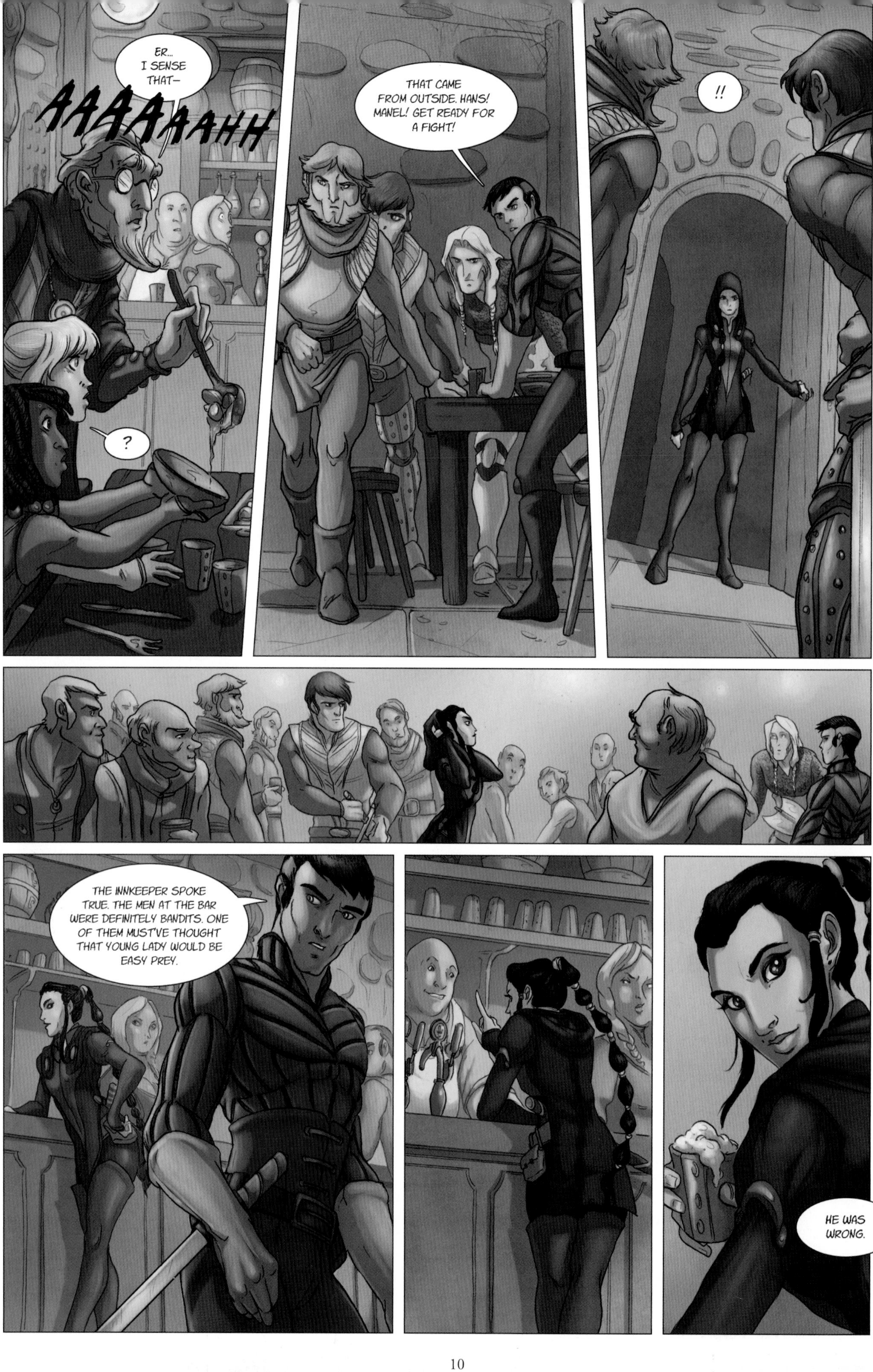
ER... I SENSE THAT—
AAAAAAAHH
?
THAT CAME FROM OUTSIDE. HANS! MANEL! GET READY FOR A FIGHT!
!!
THE INNKEEPER SPOKE TRUE. THE MEN AT THE BAR WERE DEFINITELY BANDITS. ONE OF THEM MUST'VE THOUGHT THAT YOUNG LADY WOULD BE EASY PREY.
HE WAS WRONG.

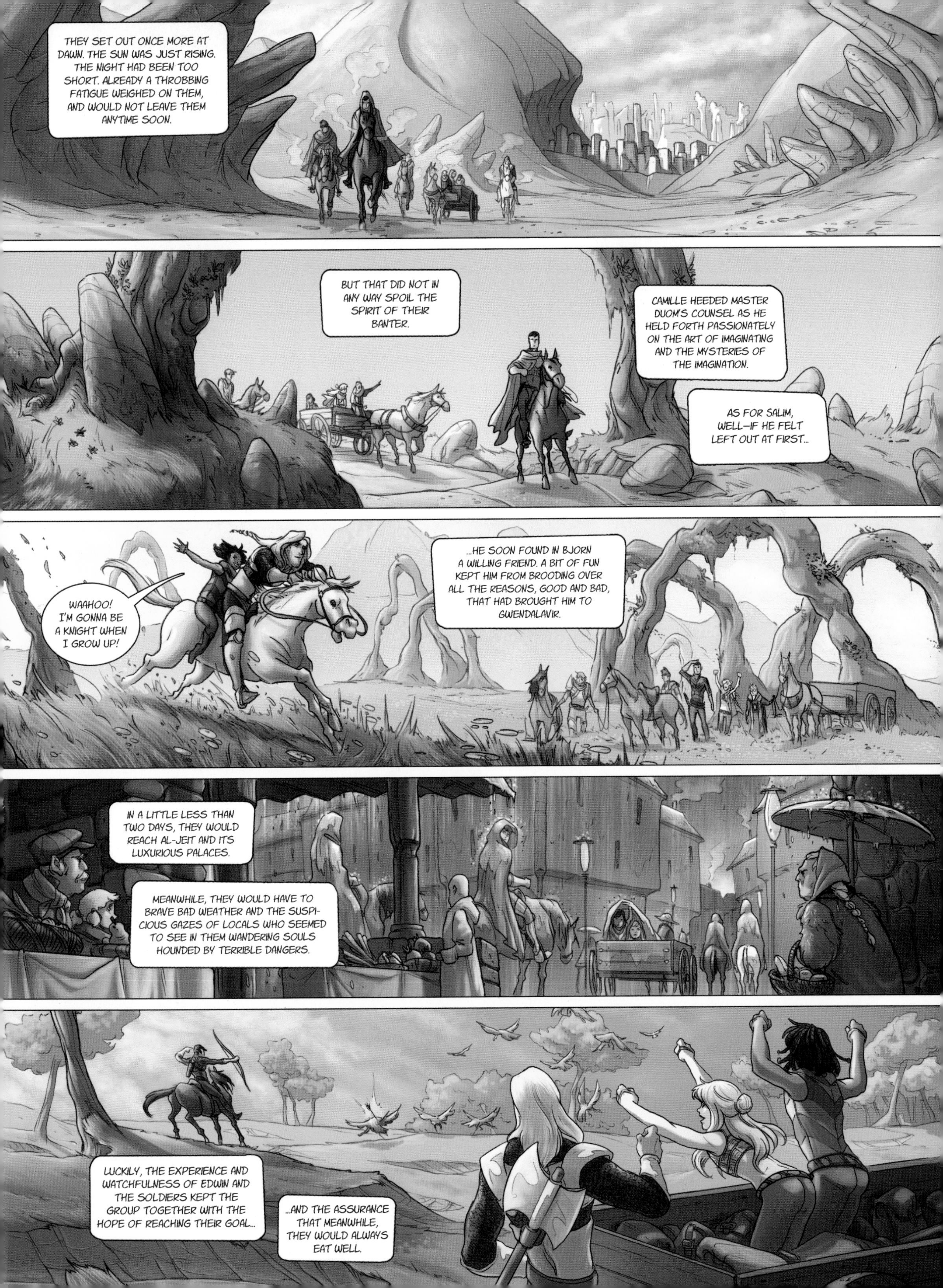
THEY SET OUT ONCE MORE AT DAWN. THE SUN WAS JUST RISING. THE NIGHT HAD BEEN TOO SHORT. ALREADY A THROBBING FATIGUE WEIGHED ON THEM, AND WOULD NOT LEAVE THEM ANYTIME SOON.
BUT THAT DID NOT IN ANY WAY SPOIL THE SPIRIT OF THEIR BANTER.
CAMILLE HEEDED MASTER DUOM'S COUNSEL AS HE HELD FORTH PASSIONATELY ON THE ART OF IMAGINATING AND THE MYSTERIES OF THE IMAGINATION.
AS FOR SALIM, WELL—IF HE FELT LEFT OUT AT FIRST...
WAAHOO! I'M GONNA BE A KNIGHT WHEN I GROW UP!
...HE SOON FOUND IN BJORN A WILLING FRIEND. A BIT OF FUN KEPT HIM FROM BROODING OVER ALL THE REASONS, GOOD AND BAD, THAT HAD BROUGHT HIM TO GWENDALAVIR.
IN A LITTLE LESS THAN TWO DAYS, THEY WOULD REACH AL-JEIT AND ITS LUXURIOUS PALACES.
MEANWHILE, THEY WOULD HAVE TO BRAVE BAD WEATHER AND THE SUSPICIOUS GAZES OF LOCALS WHO SEEMED TO SEE IN THEM WANDERING SOULS HOUNDED BY TERRIBLE DANGERS.
LUCKILY, THE EXPERIENCE AND WATCHFULNESS OF EDWIN AND THE SOLDIERS KEPT THE GROUP TOGETHER WITH THE HOPE OF REACHING THEIR GOAL...
...AND THE ASSURANCE THAT MEANWHILE, THEY WOULD ALWAYS EAT WELL.

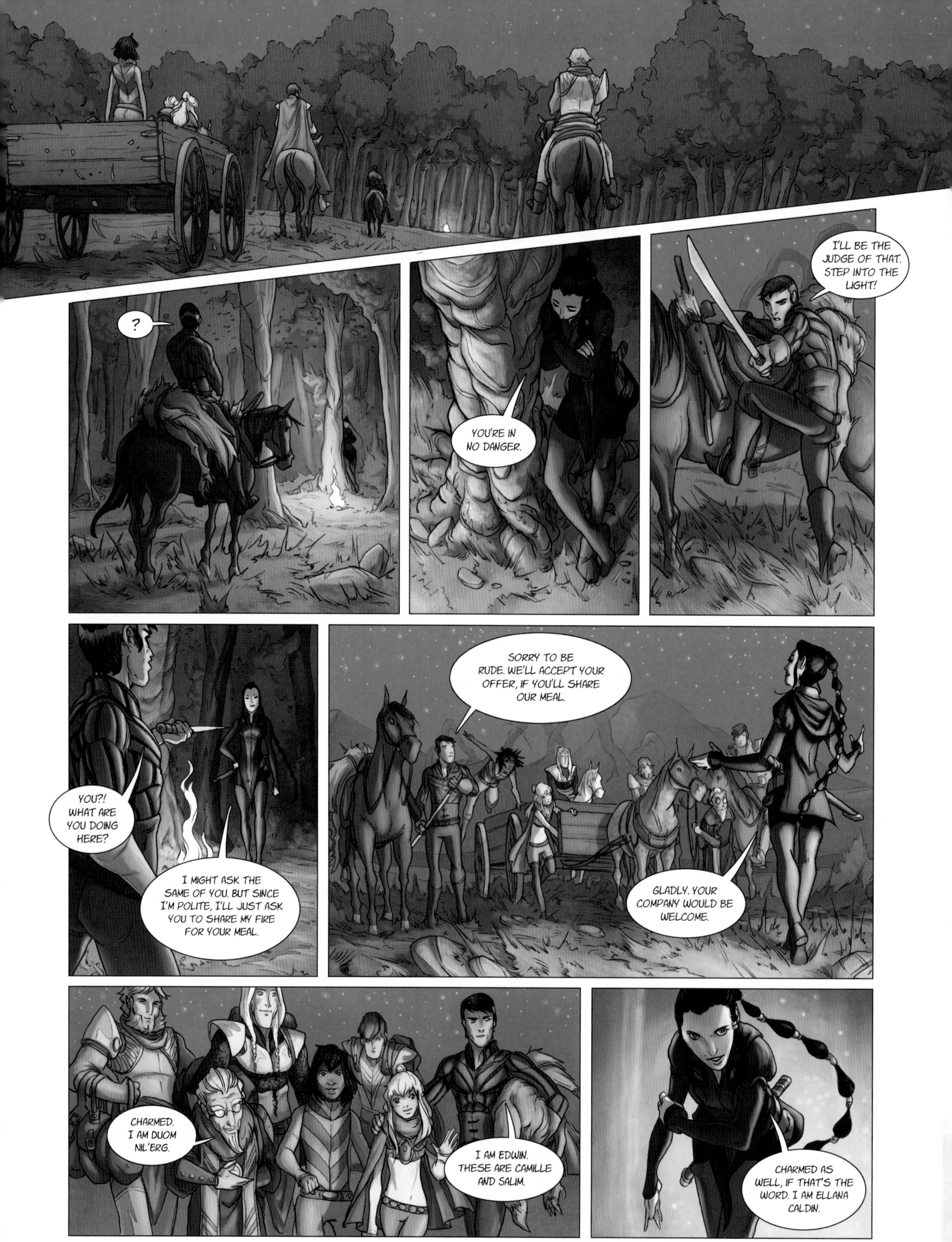
?
YOU'RE IN NO DANGER.
I'LL BE THE JUDGE OF THAT. STEP INTO THE LIGHT!
YOU?! WHAT ARE YOU DOING HERE?
I MIGHT ASK THE SAME OF YOU. BUT SINCE I'M POLITE, I'LL JUST ASK YOU TO SHARE MY FIRE FOR YOUR MEAL.
SORRY TO BE RUDE. WE'LL ACCEPT YOUR OFFER, IF YOU'LL SHARE OUR MEAL.
GLADLY. YOUR COMPANY WOULD BE WELCOME.
CHARMED. I AM DUOM NIL'ERG.
I AM EDWIN. THESE ARE CAMILLE AND SALIM.
CHARMED AS WELL, IF THAT'S THE WORD. I AM ELLANA CALDIN.

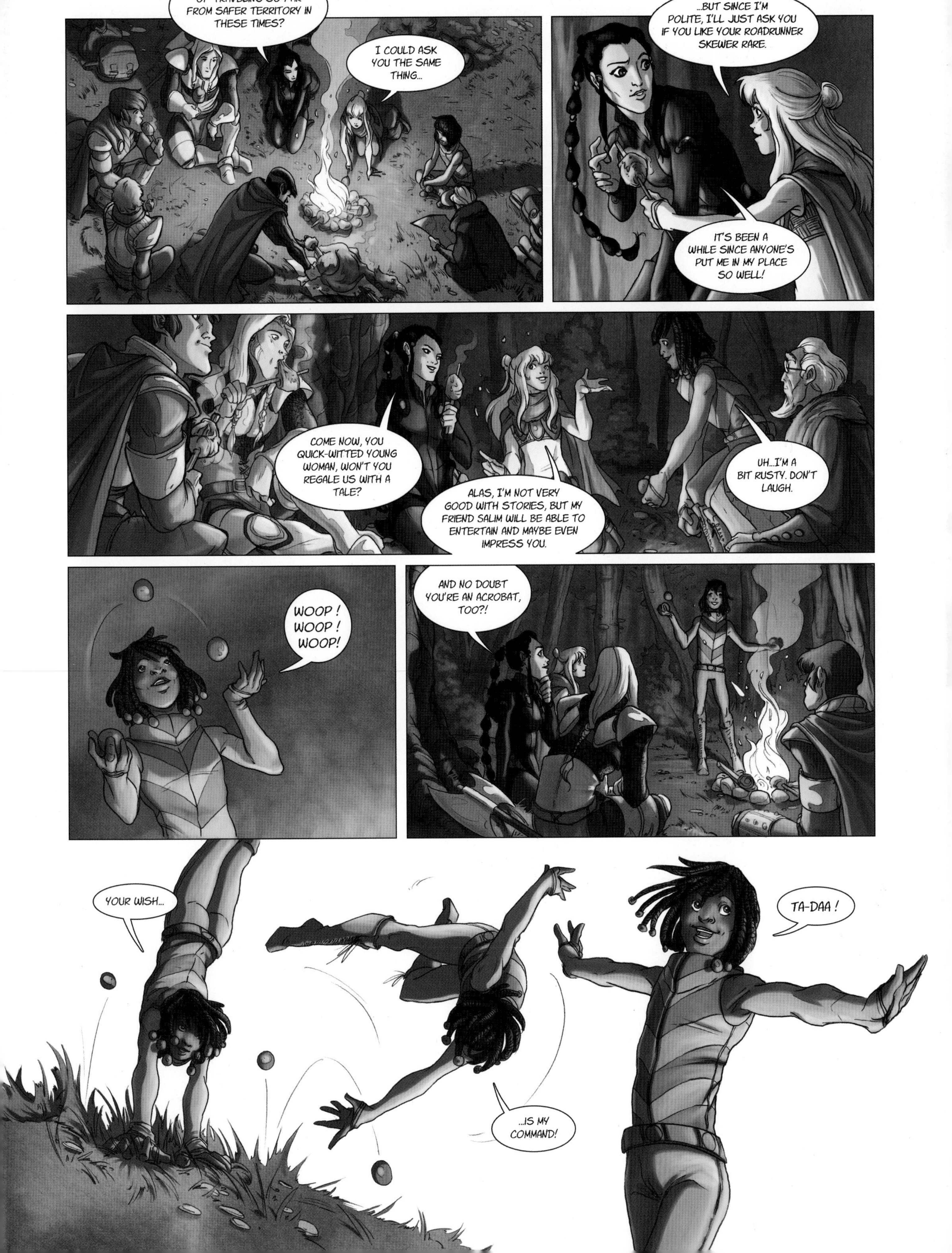
AREN'T YOU AFRAID OF TRAVELING SO FAR FROM SAFER TERRITORY IN THESE TIMES?
I COULD ASK YOU THE SAME THING...
...BUT SINCE I'M POLITE, I'LL JUST ASK YOU IF YOU LIKE YOUR ROADRUNNER SKEWER RARE.
IT'S BEEN A WHILE SINCE ANYONE'S PUT ME IN MY PLACE SO WELL!
COME NOW, YOU QUICK-WITTED YOUNG WOMAN, WON'T YOU REGALE US WITH A TALE?
ALAS, I'M NOT VERY GOOD WITH STORIES, BUT MY FRIEND SALIM WILL BE ABLE TO ENTERTAIN AND MAYBE EVEN IMPRESS YOU.
UH...I'M A BIT RUSTY. DON'T LAUGH.
WOOP! WOOP! WOOP!
AND NO DOUBT YOU'RE AN ACROBAT, TOO?!
YOUR WISH...
...IS MY COMMAND!
TA-DAA!

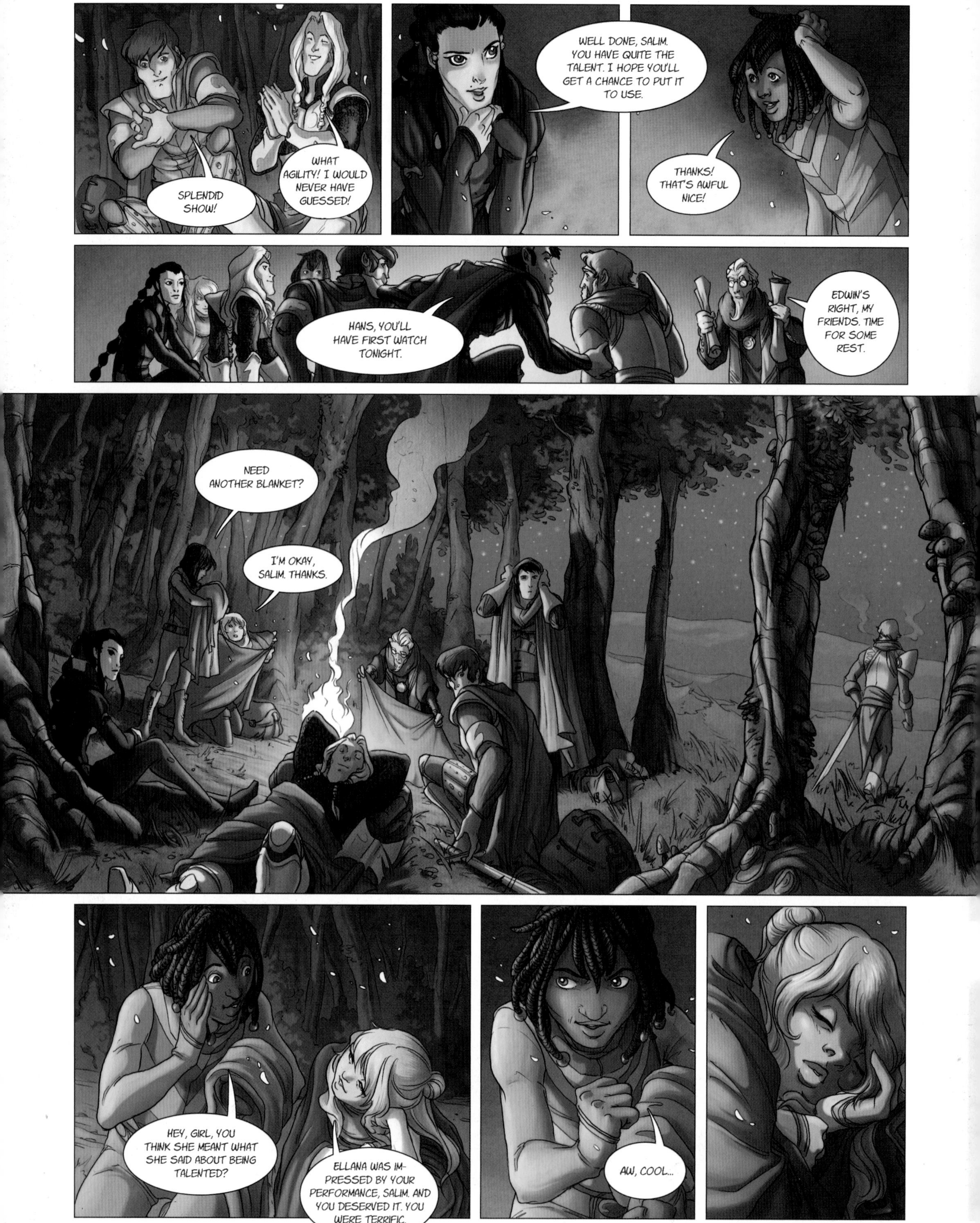
SPLENDID SHOW!
WHAT AGILITY! I WOULD NEVER HAVE GUESSED!
WELL DONE, SALIM. YOU HAVE QUITE THE TALENT. I HOPE YOU'LL GET A CHANCE TO PUT IT TO USE.
THANKS! THAT'S AWFUL NICE!
HANS, YOU'LL HAVE FIRST WATCH TONIGHT.
EDWIN'S RIGHT, MY FRIENDS. TIME FOR SOME REST.
NEED ANOTHER BLANKET?
I'M OKAY, SALIM. THANKS.
HEY, GIRL, YOU THINK SHE MEANT WHAT SHE SAID ABOUT BEING TALENTED?
ELLANA WAS IMPRESSED BY YOUR PERFORMANCE, SALIM. AND YOU DESERVED IT. YOU WERE TERRIFIC.
AW, COOL...

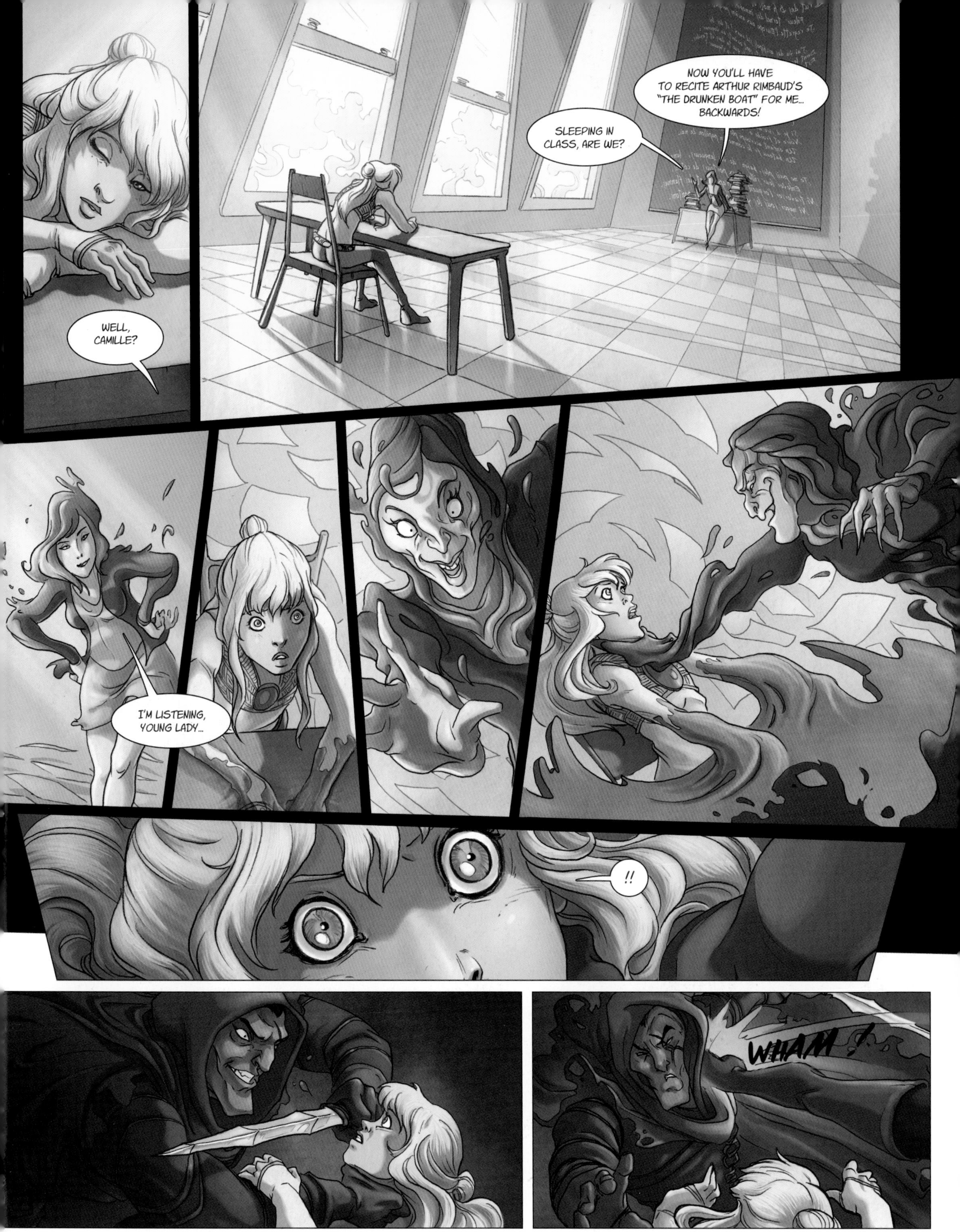

SLEEPING IN CLASS, ARE WE?
NOW YOU'LL HAVE TO RECITE ARTHUR RIMBAUD'S "THE DRUNKEN BOAT" FOR ME... BACKWARDS!
WELL, CAMILLE?
I'M LISTENING, YOUNG LADY...
!!
WHAM!

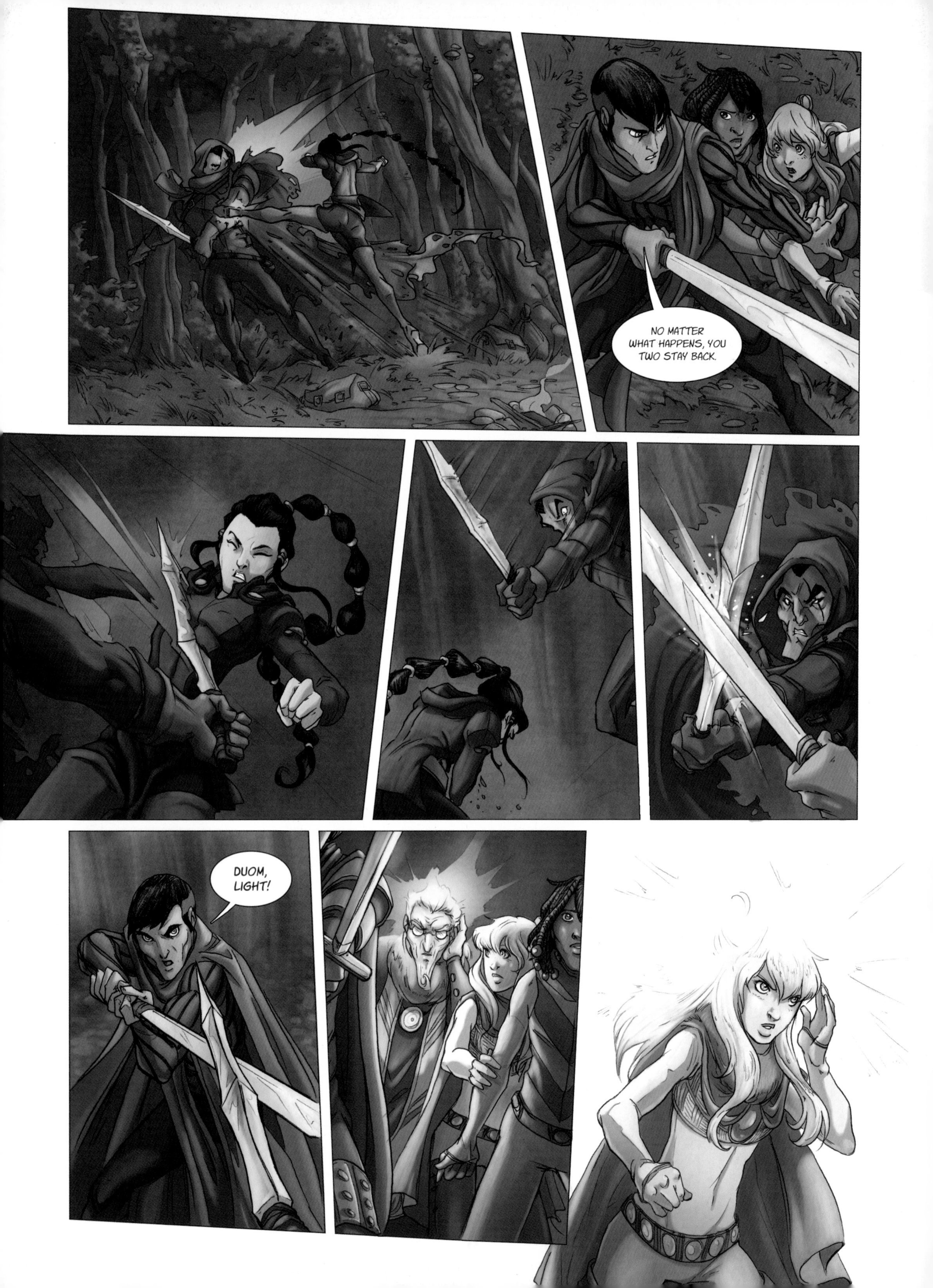

NO MATTER WHAT HAPPENS, YOU TWO STAY BACK.
DUOM, LIGHT!

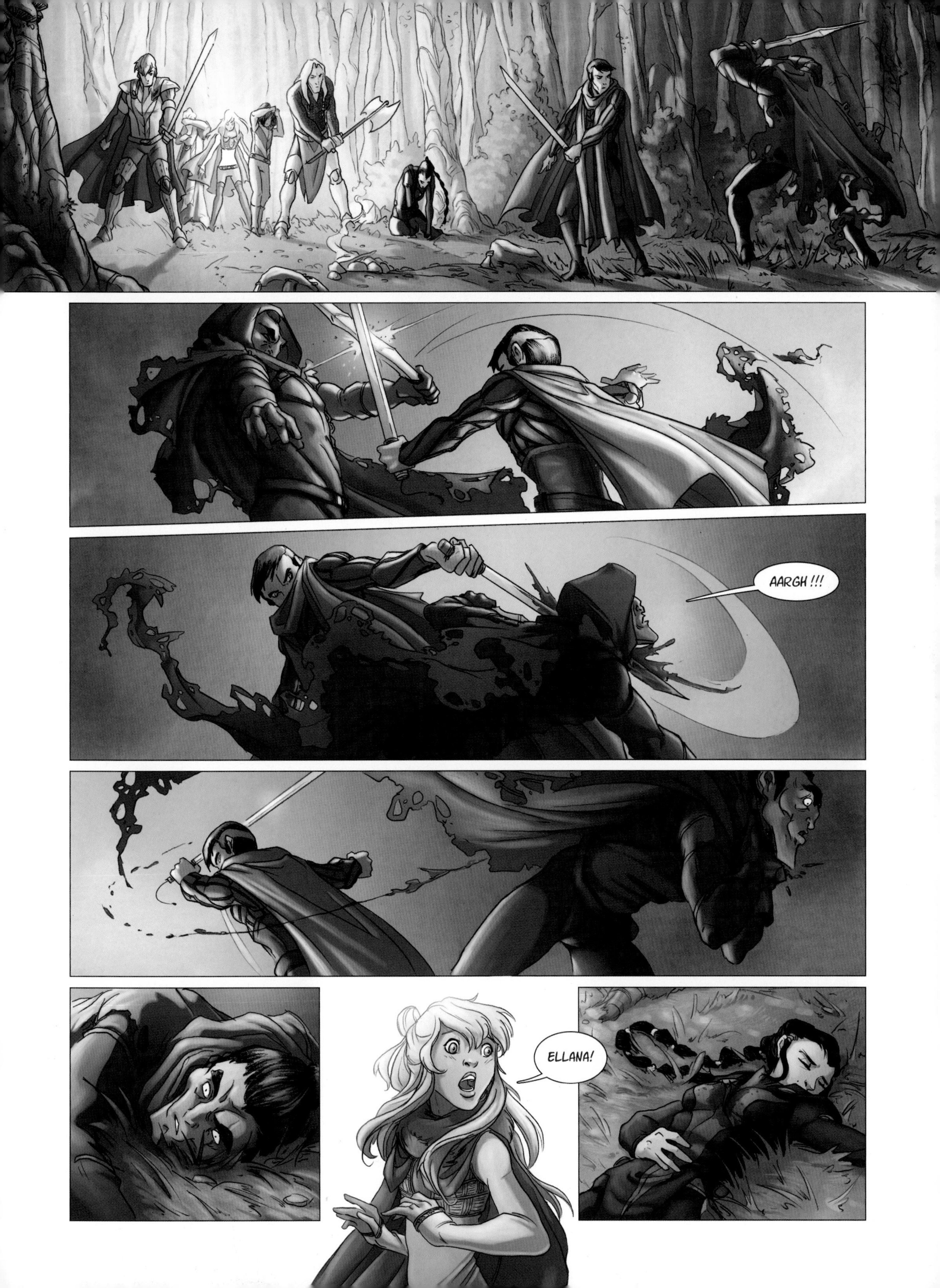
AARGH !!!
ELLANA!

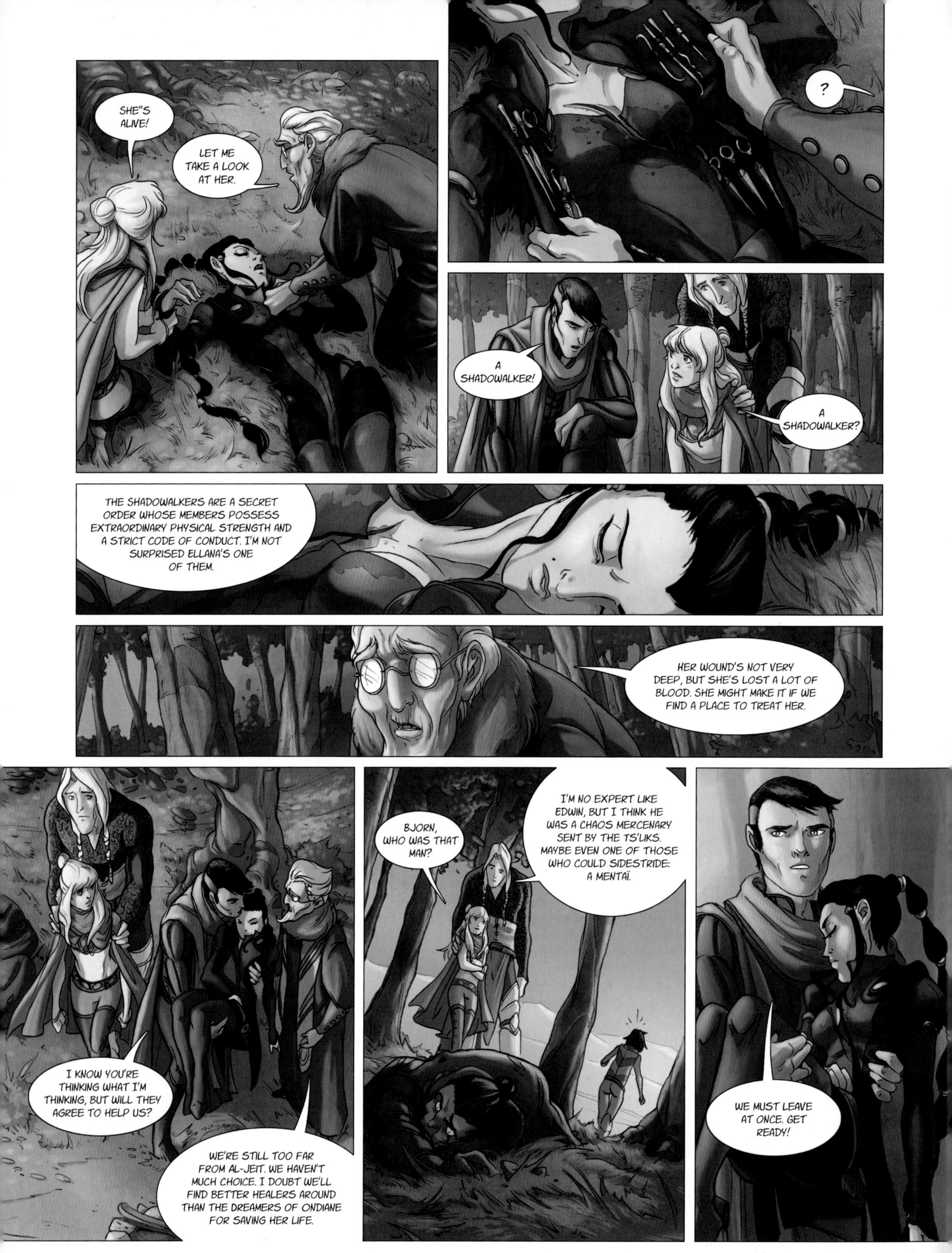
SHE"S ALIVE!
LET ME TAKE A LOOK AT HER.
?
A SHADOWALKER!
A SHADOWALKER?
THE SHADOWALKERS ARE A SECRET ORDER WHOSE MEMBERS POSSESS EXTRAORDINARY PHYSICAL STRENGTH AND A STRICT CODE OF CONDUCT. I'M NOT SURPRISED ELLANA'S ONE OF THEM.
HER WOUND'S NOT VERY DEEP, BUT SHE'S LOST A LOT OF BLOOD. SHE MIGHT MAKE IT IF WE FIND A PLACE TO TREAT HER.
I KNOW YOU'RE THINKING WHAT I'M THINKING, BUT WILL THEY AGREE TO HELP US?
WE'RE STILL TOO FAR FROM AL-JEIT. WE HAVEN'T MUCH CHOICE. I DOUBT WE'LL FIND BETTER HEALERS AROUND THAN THE DREAMERS OF ONDIANE FOR SAVING HER LIFE.
BJORN, WHO WAS THAT MAN?
I'M NO EXPERT LIKE EDWIN, BUT I THINK HE WAS A CHAOS MERCENARY SENT BY THE TS'LIKS. MAYBE EVEN ONE OF THOSE WHO COULD SIDESTRIDE: A MENTAÏ.
WE MUST LEAVE AT ONCE. GET READY!

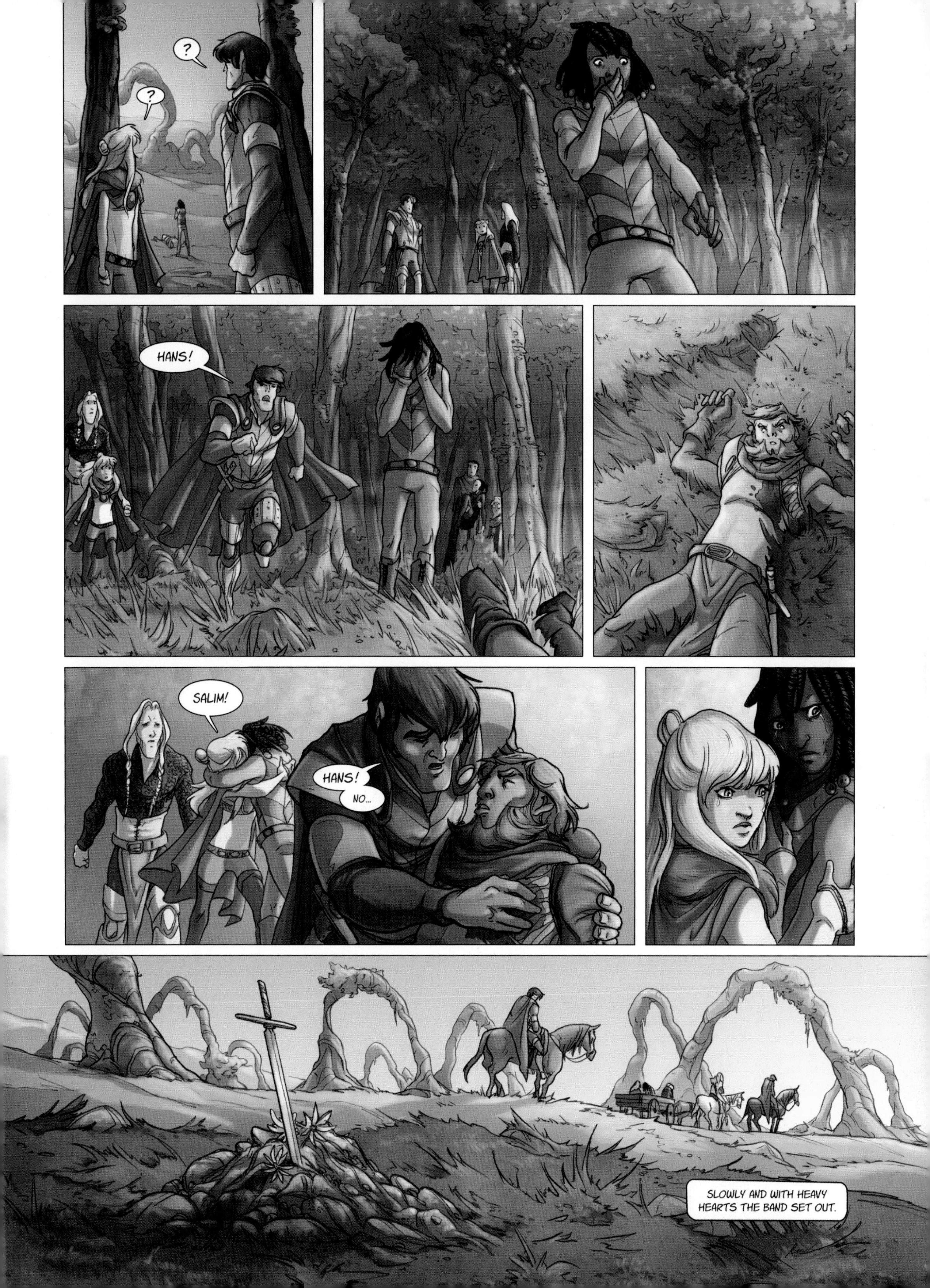
?
?
HANS!
SALIM!
HANS!
NO...
SLOWLY AND WITH HEAVY HEARTS THE BAND SET OUT.

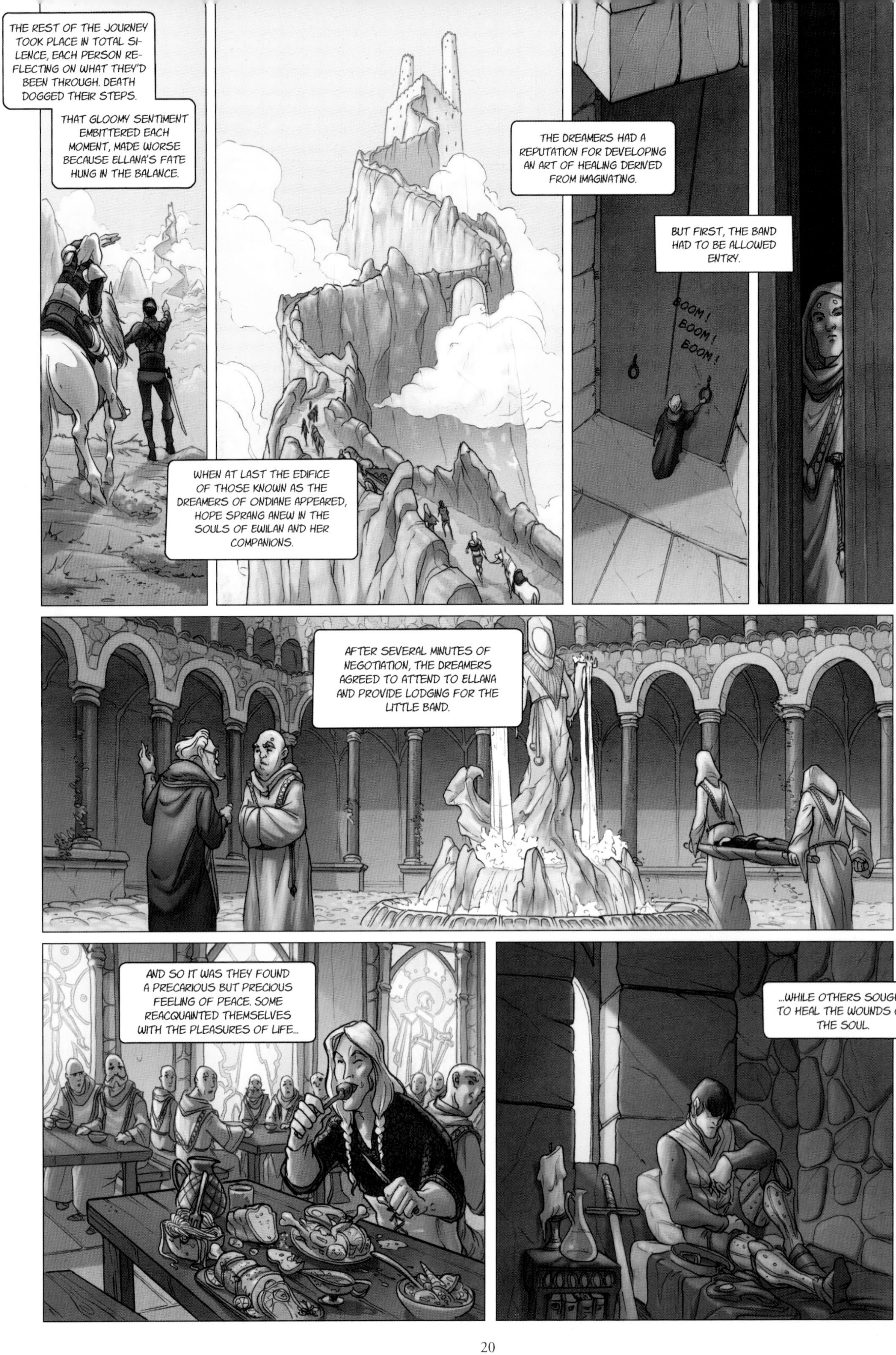

THE REST OF THE JOURNEY TOOK PLACE IN TOTAL SILENCE, EACH PERSON REFLECTING ON WHAT THEY'D BEEN THROUGH. DEATH DOGGED THEIR STEPS.
THAT GLOOMY SENTIMENT EMBITTERED EACH MOMENT, MADE WORSE BECAUSE ELLANA'S FATE HUNG IN THE BALANCE.
WHEN AT LAST THE EDIFICE OF THOSE KNOWN AS THE DREAMERS OF ONDIANE APPEARED, HOPE SPRANG ANEW IN THE SOULS OF EWILAN AND HER COMPANIONS.
THE DREAMERS HAD A REPUTATION FOR DEVELOPING AN ART OF HEALING DERIVED FROM IMAGINATING.
BUT FIRST, THE BAND HAD TO BE ALLOWED ENTRY.
BOOM! BOOM! BOOM!
AFTER SEVERAL MINUTES OF NEGOTIATION, THE DREAMERS AGREED TO ATTEND TO ELLANA AND PROVIDE LODGING FOR THE LITTLE BAND.
AND SO IT WAS THEY FOUND A PRECARIOUS BUT PRECIOUS FEELING OF PEACE. SOME REACQUAINTED THEMSELVES WITH THE PLEASURES OF LIFE...
...WHILE OTHERS SOUGHT TO HEAL THE WOUNDS OF THE SOUL.

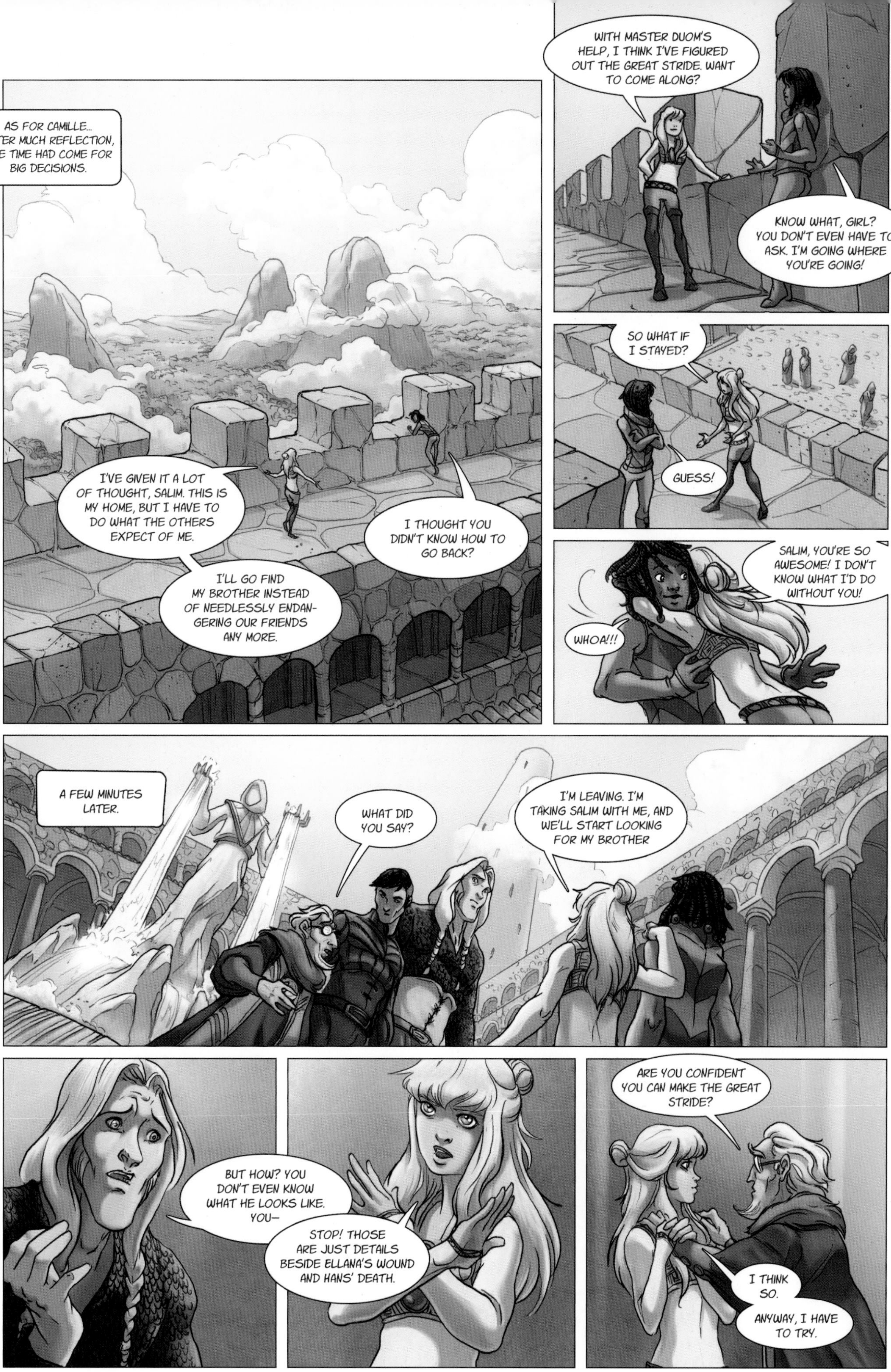
AS FOR CAMILLE... AFTER MUCH REFLECTION, THE TIME HAD COME FOR BIG DECISIONS.
I'VE GIVEN IT A LOT OF THOUGHT, SALIM. THIS IS MY HOME, BUT I HAVE TO DO WHAT THE OTHERS EXPECT OF ME.
I'LL GO FIND MY BROTHER INSTEAD OF NEEDLESSLY ENDANGERING OUR FRIENDS ANY MORE.
I THOUGHT YOU DIDN'T KNOW HOW TO GO BACK?
WITH MASTER DUOM'S HELP, I THINK I'VE FIGURED OUT THE GREAT STRIDE. WANT TO COME ALONG?
KNOW WHAT, GIRL? YOU DON'T EVEN HAVE TO ASK. I'M GOING WHERE YOU'RE GOING!
SO WHAT IF I STAYED?
GUESS!
SALIM, YOU'RE SO AWESOME! I DON'T KNOW WHAT I'D DO WITHOUT YOU!
WHOA!!!
A FEW MINUTES LATER.
WHAT DID YOU SAY?
I'M LEAVING. I'M TAKING SALIM WITH ME, AND WE'LL START LOOKING FOR MY BROTHER
BUT HOW? YOU DON'T EVEN KNOW WHAT HE LOOKS LIKE. YOU—
STOP! THOSE ARE JUST DETAILS BESIDE ELLANA'S WOUND AND HANS' DEATH.
ARE YOU CONFIDENT YOU CAN MAKE THE GREAT STRIDE?
I THINK SO.
ANYWAY, I HAVE TO TRY.

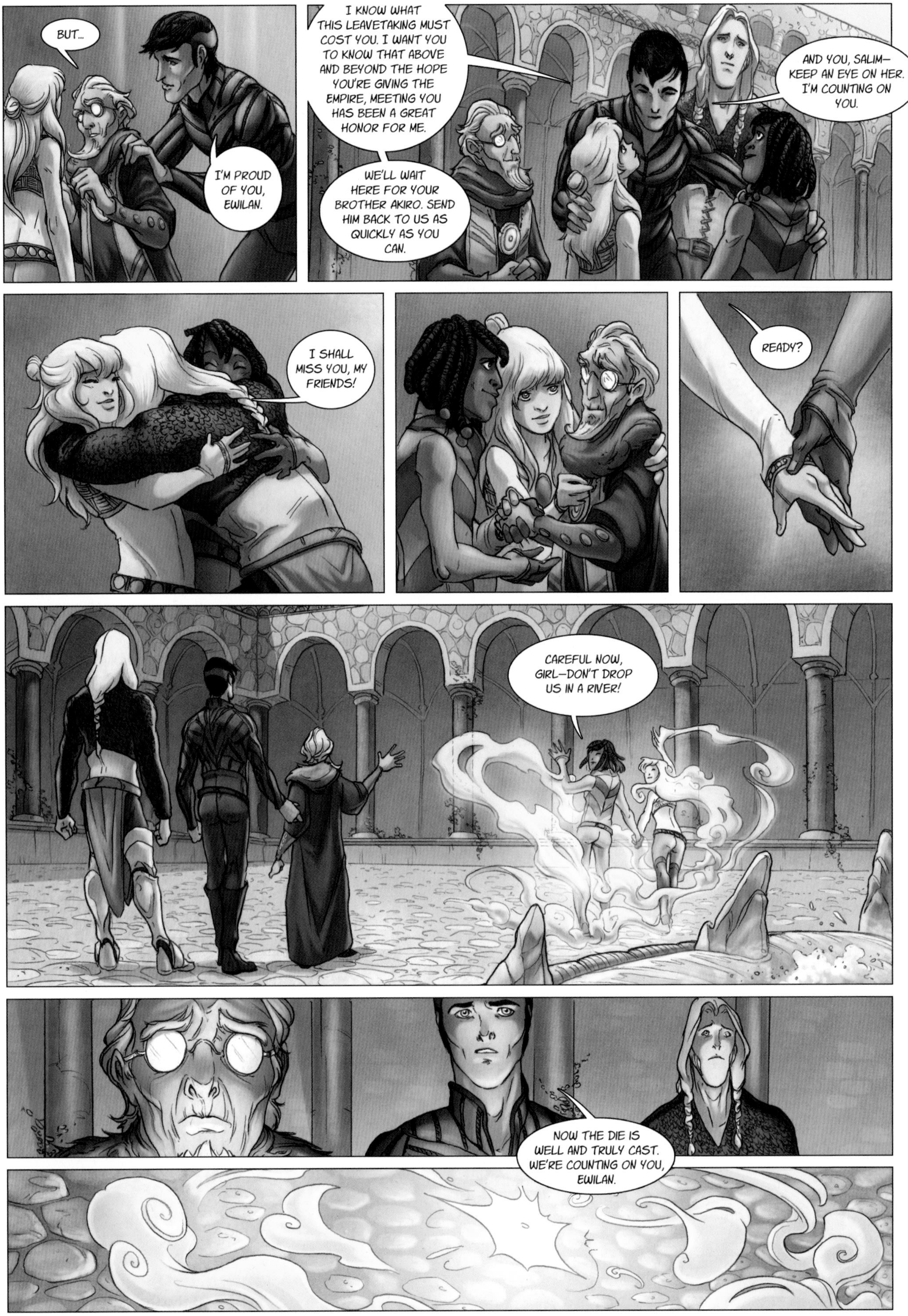
BUT...
I'M PROUD OF YOU, EWILAN.
I KNOW WHAT THIS LEAVETAKING MUST COST YOU. I WANT YOU TO KNOW THAT ABOVE AND BEYOND THE HOPE YOU'RE GIVING THE EMPIRE, MEETING YOU HAS BEEN A GREAT HONOR FOR ME.
WE'LL WAIT HERE FOR YOUR BROTHER AKIRO. SEND HIM BACK TO US AS QUICKLY AS YOU CAN.
AND YOU, SALIM— KEEP AN EYE ON HER. I'M COUNTING ON YOU.
I SHALL MISS YOU, MY FRIENDS!
READY?
CAREFUL NOW, GIRL—DON'T DROP US IN A RIVER!
NOW THE DIE IS WELL AND TRULY CAST. WE'RE COUNTING ON YOU, EWILAN.

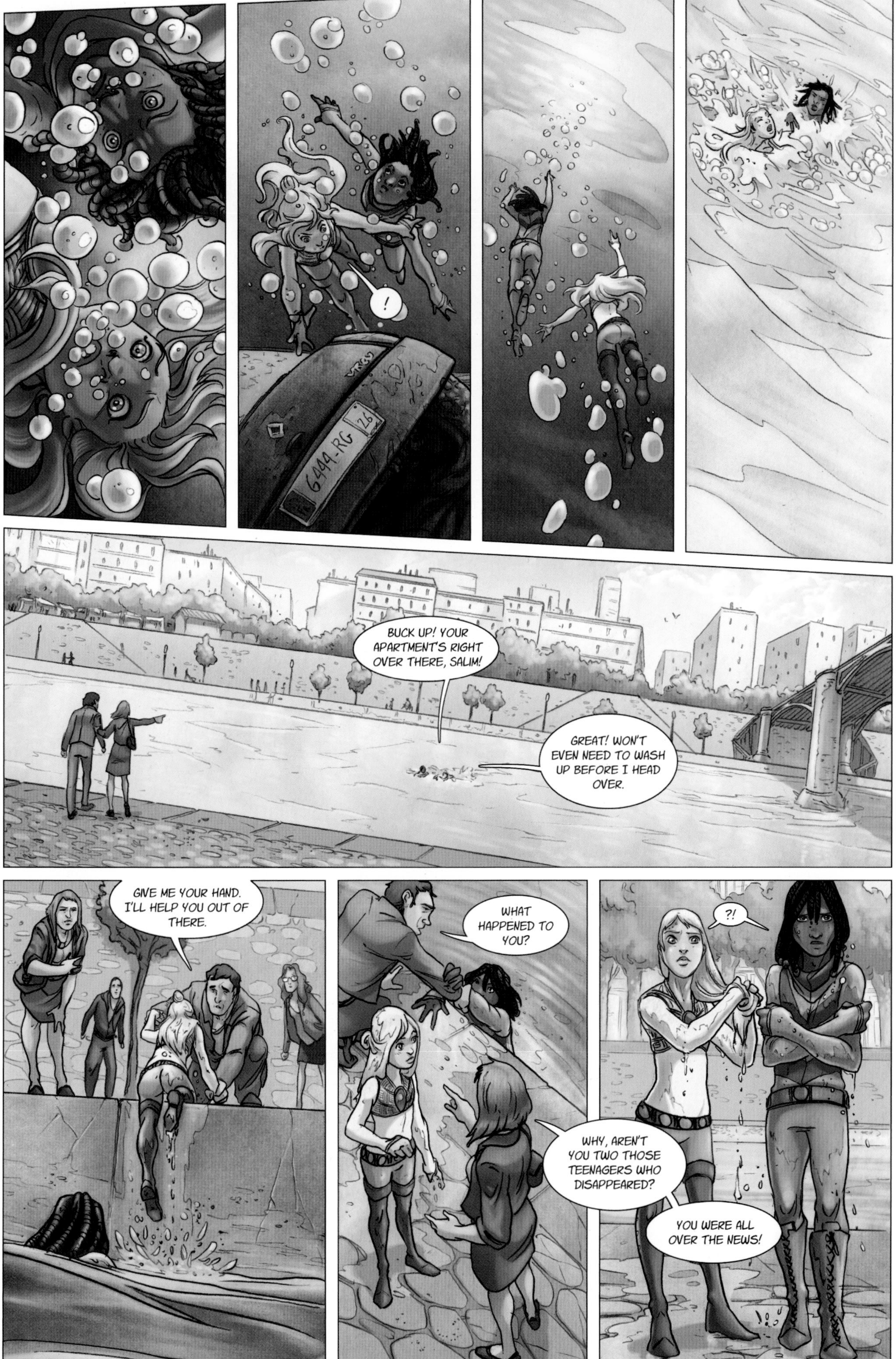
!
6444.RG 26
BUCK UP! YOUR APARTMENT'S RIGHT OVER THERE, SALIM!
GREAT! WON'T EVEN NEED TO WASH UP BEFORE I HEAD OVER.
GIVE ME YOUR HAND. I'LL HELP YOU OUT OF THERE.
WHAT HAPPENED TO YOU?
WHY, AREN'T YOU TWO THOSE TEENAGERS WHO DISAPPEARED?
YOU WERE ALL OVER THE NEWS!
?!

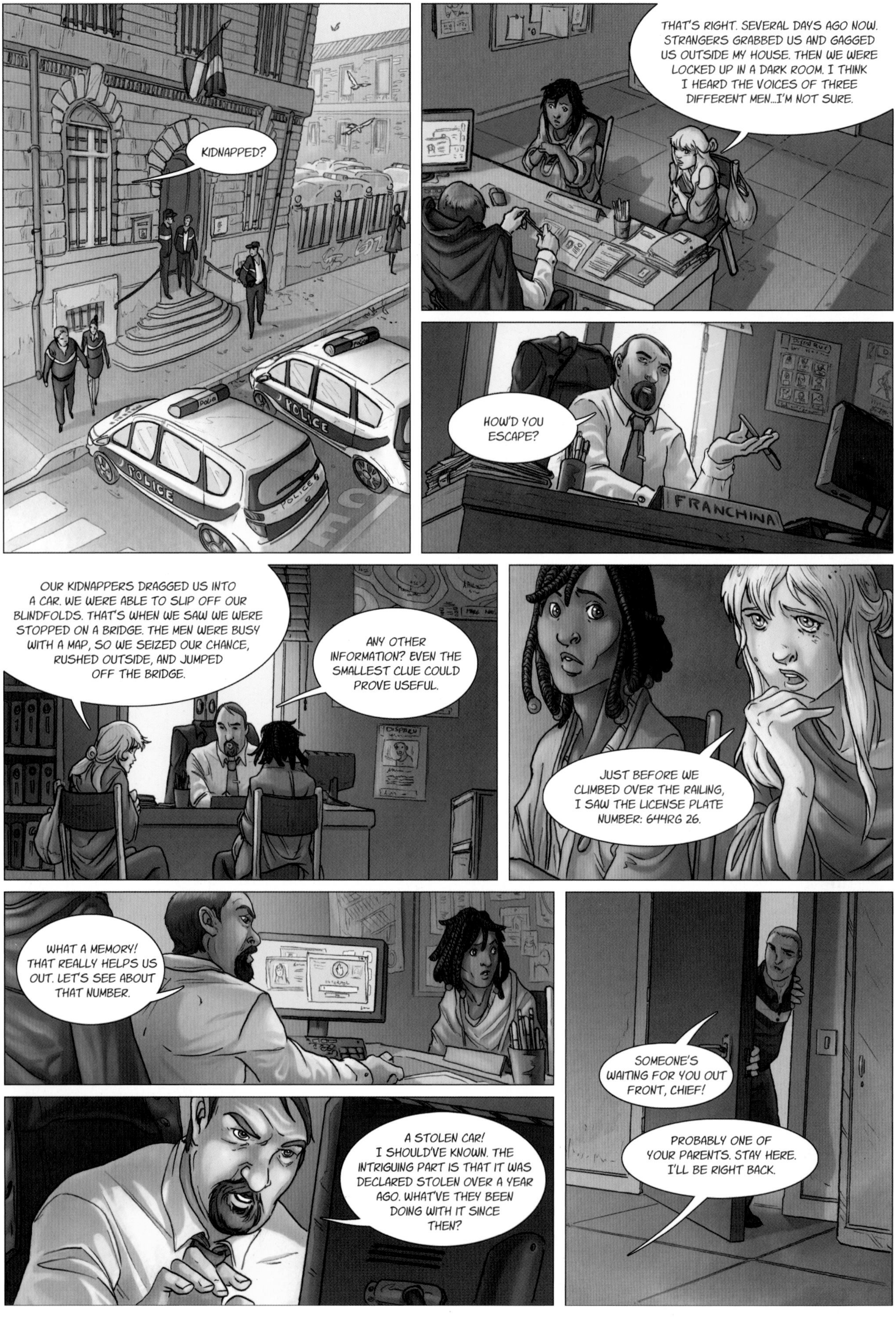
KIDNAPPED?
THAT'S RIGHT. SEVERAL DAYS AGO NOW. STRANGERS GRABBED US AND GAGGED US OUTSIDE MY HOUSE. THEN WE WERE LOCKED UP IN A DARK ROOM. I THINK I HEARD THE VOICES OF THREE DIFFERENT MEN...I'M NOT SURE.
HOW'D YOU ESCAPE?
FRANCHINA
OUR KIDNAPPERS DRAGGED US INTO A CAR. WE WERE ABLE TO SLIP OFF OUR BLINDFOLDS. THAT'S WHEN WE SAW WE WERE STOPPED ON A BRIDGE. THE MEN WERE BUSY WITH A MAP, SO WE SEIZED OUR CHANCE, RUSHED OUTSIDE, AND JUMPED OFF THE BRIDGE.
ANY OTHER INFORMATION? EVEN THE SMALLEST CLUE COULD PROVE USEFUL.
JUST BEFORE WE CLIMBED OVER THE RAILING, I SAW THE LICENSE PLATE NUMBER: 644RG 26.
WHAT A MEMORY! THAT REALLY HELPS US OUT. LET'S SEE ABOUT THAT NUMBER.
A STOLEN CAR! I SHOULD'VE KNOWN. THE INTRIGUING PART IS THAT IT WAS DECLARED STOLEN OVER A YEAR AGO. WHAT'VE THEY BEEN DOING WITH IT SINCE THEN?
SOMEONE'S WAITING FOR YOU OUT FRONT, CHIEF!
PROBABLY ONE OF YOUR PARENTS. STAY HERE. I'LL BE RIGHT BACK.

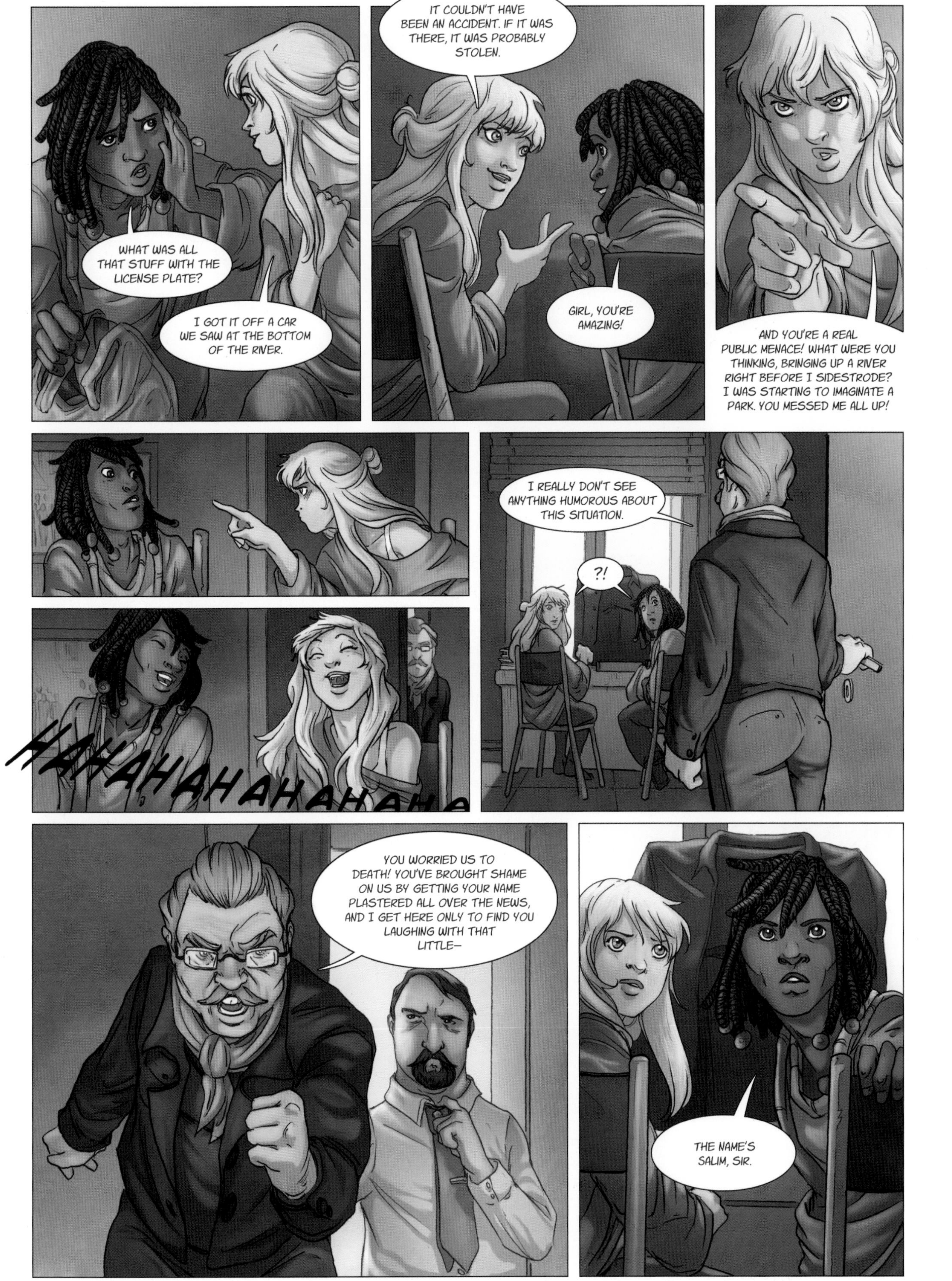
WHAT WAS ALL THAT STUFF WITH THE LICENSE PLATE?
I GOT IT OFF A CAR WE SAW AT THE BOTTOM OF THE RIVER.
IT COULDN'T HAVE BEEN AN ACCIDENT. IF IT WAS THERE, IT WAS PROBABLY STOLEN.
GIRL, YOU'RE AMAZING!
AND YOU'RE A REAL PUBLIC MENACE! WHAT WERE YOU THINKING, BRINGING UP A RIVER RIGHT BEFORE I SIDESTRODE? I WAS STARTING TO IMAGINATE A PARK. YOU MESSED ME ALL UP!
HAHAHAHAHAHAHAHA
I REALLY DON'T SEE ANYTHING HUMOROUS ABOUT THIS SITUATION.
?!
YOU WORRIED US TO DEATH! YOU'VE BROUGHT SHAME ON US BY GETTING YOUR NAME PLASTERED ALL OVER THE NEWS, AND I GET HERE ONLY TO FIND YOU LAUGHING WITH THAT LITTLE–
THE NAME'S SALIM, SIR.

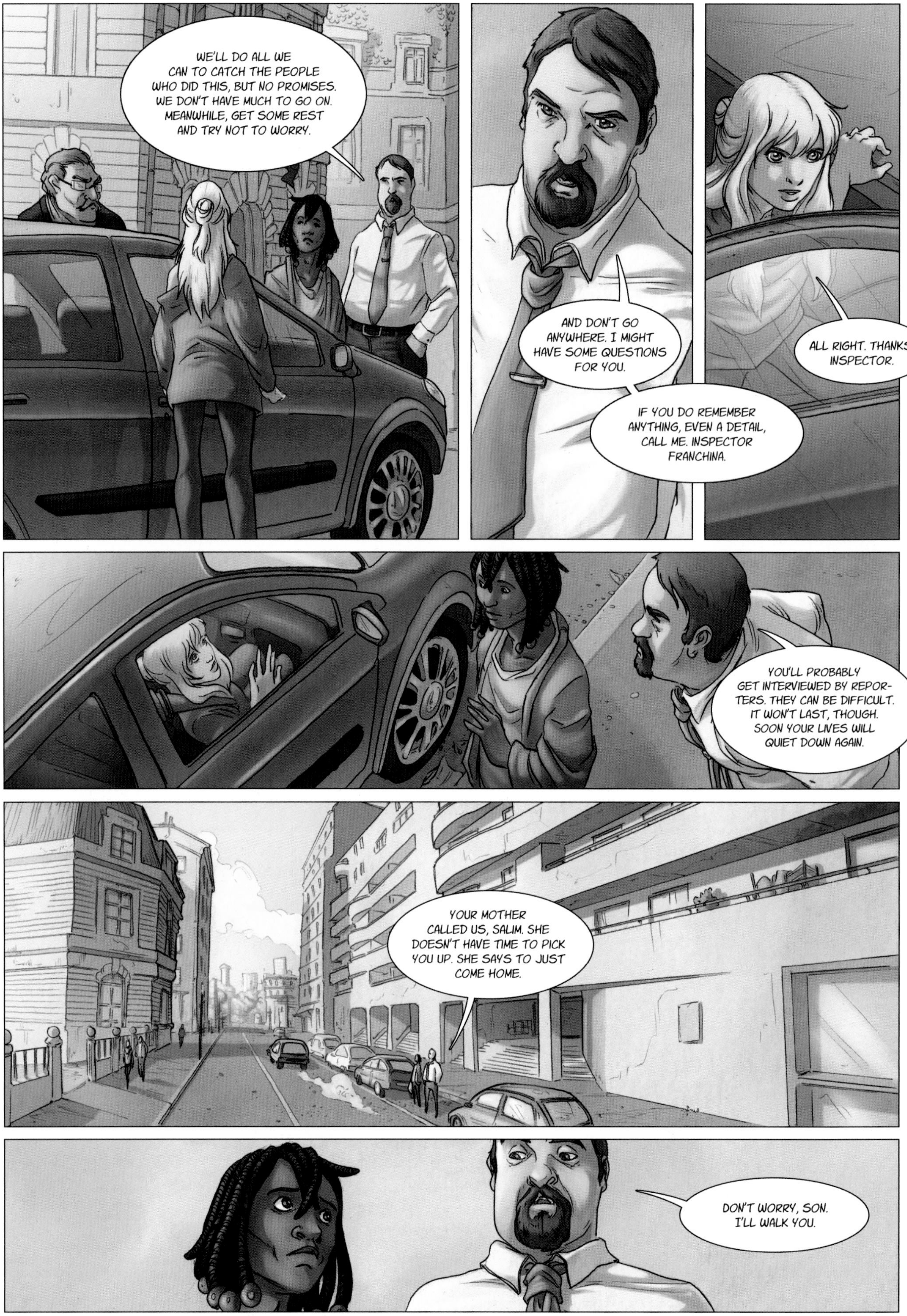
WE'LL DO ALL WE CAN TO CATCH THE PEOPLE WHO DID THIS, BUT NO PROMISES. WE DON'T HAVE MUCH TO GO ON. MEANWHILE, GET SOME REST AND TRY NOT TO WORRY.
AND DON'T GO ANYWHERE. I MIGHT HAVE SOME QUESTIONS FOR YOU.
IF YOU DO REMEMBER ANYTHING, EVEN A DETAIL, CALL ME. INSPECTOR FRANCHINA.
ALL RIGHT. THANKS, INSPECTOR.
YOU'LL PROBABLY GET INTERVIEWED BY REPORTERS. THEY CAN BE DIFFICULT. IT WON'T LAST, THOUGH. SOON YOUR LIVES WILL QUIET DOWN AGAIN.
YOUR MOTHER CALLED US, SALIM. SHE DOESN'T HAVE TIME TO PICK YOU UP. SHE SAYS TO JUST COME HOME.
DON'T WORRY, SON. I'LL WALK YOU.

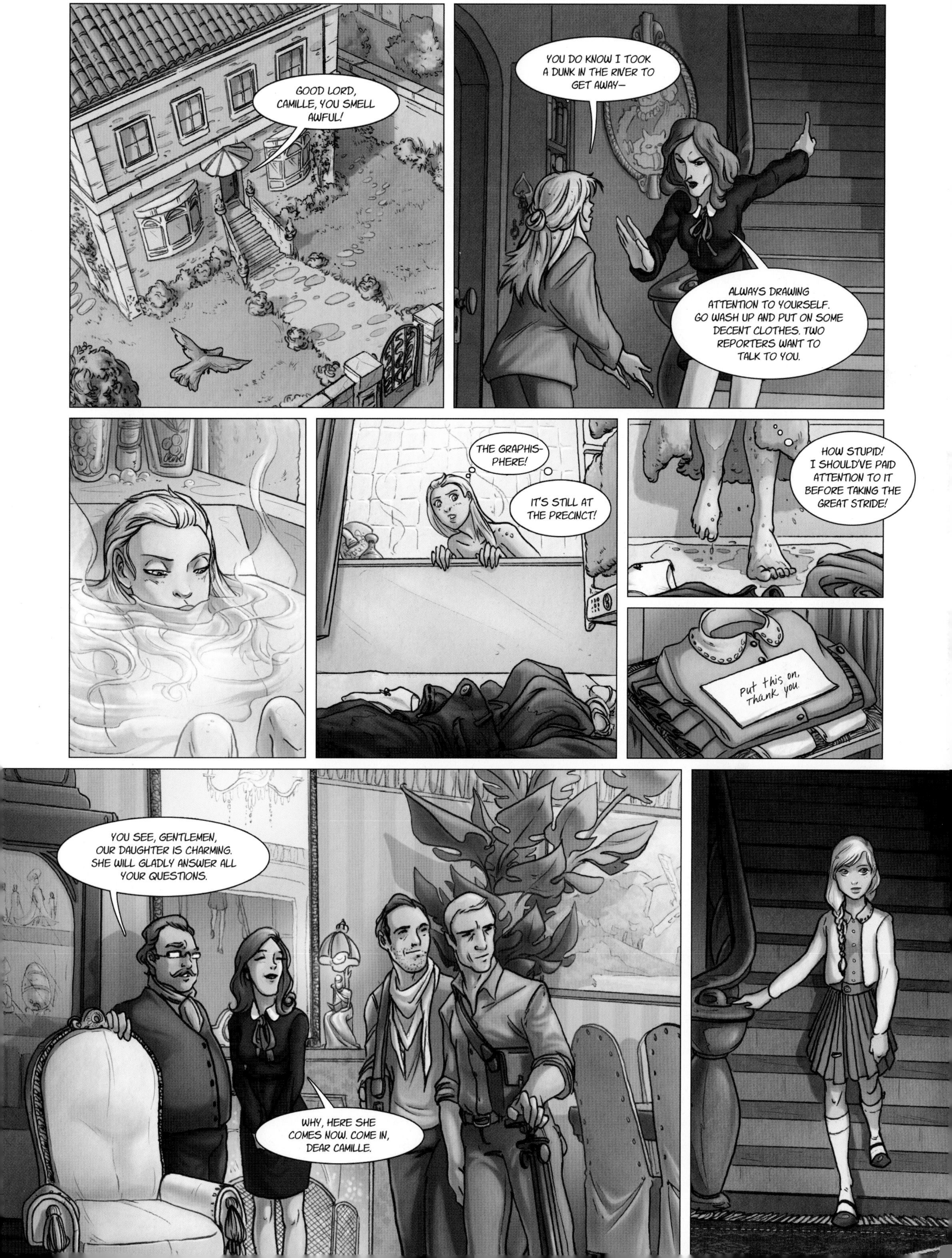
GOOD LORD, CAMILLE, YOU SMELL AWFUL!
YOU DO KNOW I TOOK A DUNK IN THE RIVER TO GET AWAY—
ALWAYS DRAWING ATTENTION TO YOURSELF. GO WASH UP AND PUT ON SOME DECENT CLOTHES. TWO REPORTERS WANT TO TALK TO YOU.
THE GRAPHIS-PHERE!
IT'S STILL AT THE PRECINCT!
HOW STUPID! I SHOULD'VE PAID ATTENTION TO IT BEFORE TAKING THE GREAT STRIDE!
Put this on, thank you.
YOU SEE, GENTLEMEN, OUR DAUGHTER IS CHARMING. SHE WILL GLADLY ANSWER ALL YOUR QUESTIONS.
WHY, HERE SHE COMES NOW. COME IN, DEAR CAMILLE.

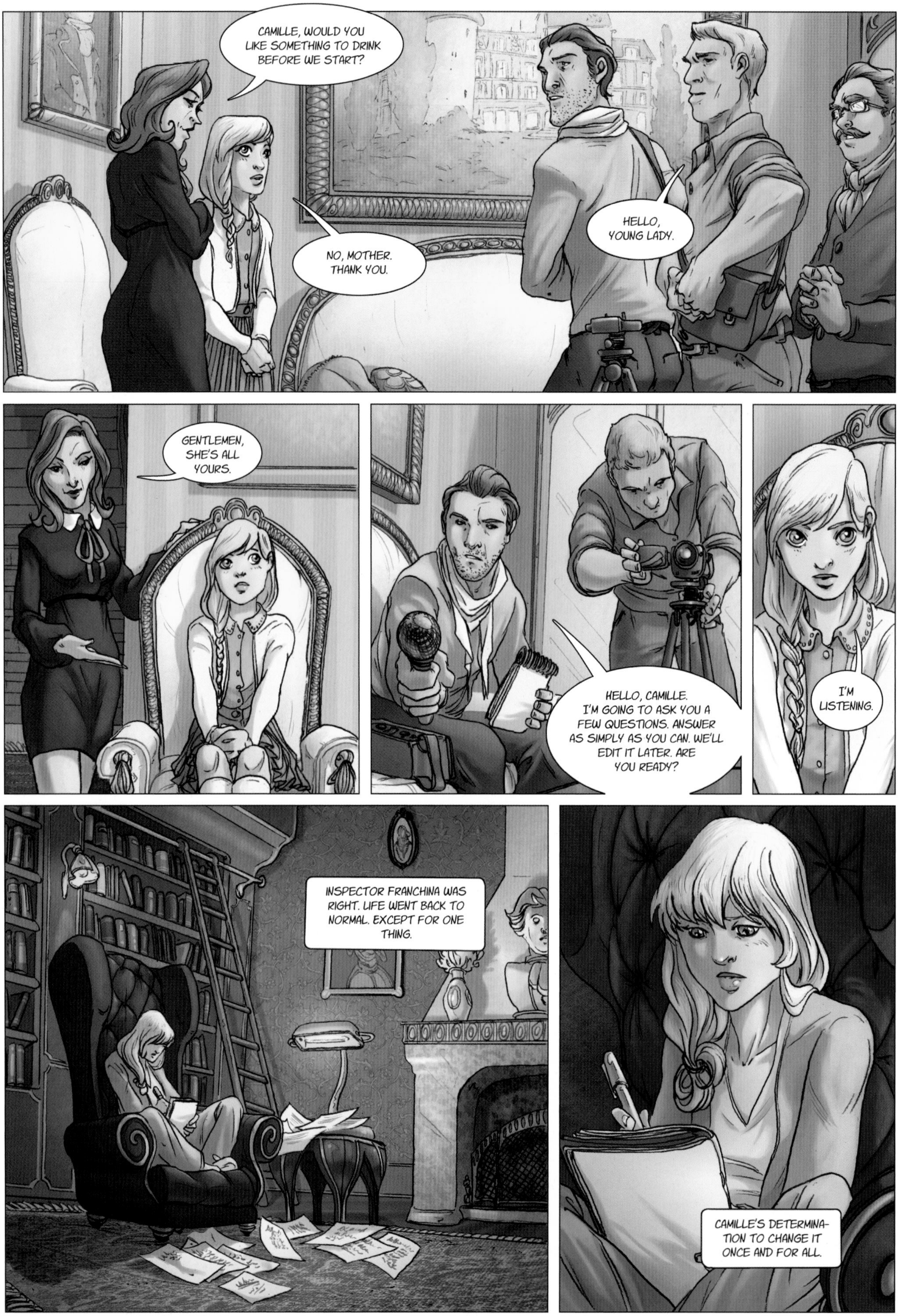
CAMILLE, WOULD YOU LIKE SOMETHING TO DRINK BEFORE WE START?
NO, MOTHER. THANK YOU.
HELLO, YOUNG LADY.
GENTLEMEN, SHE'S ALL YOURS.
HELLO, CAMILLE. I'M GOING TO ASK YOU A FEW QUESTIONS. ANSWER AS SIMPLY AS YOU CAN. WE'LL EDIT IT LATER. ARE YOU READY?
I'M LISTENING.
INSPECTOR FRANCHINA WAS RIGHT. LIFE WENT BACK TO NORMAL. EXCEPT FOR ONE THING.
CAMILLE'S DETERMINATION TO CHANGE IT ONCE AND FOR ALL.

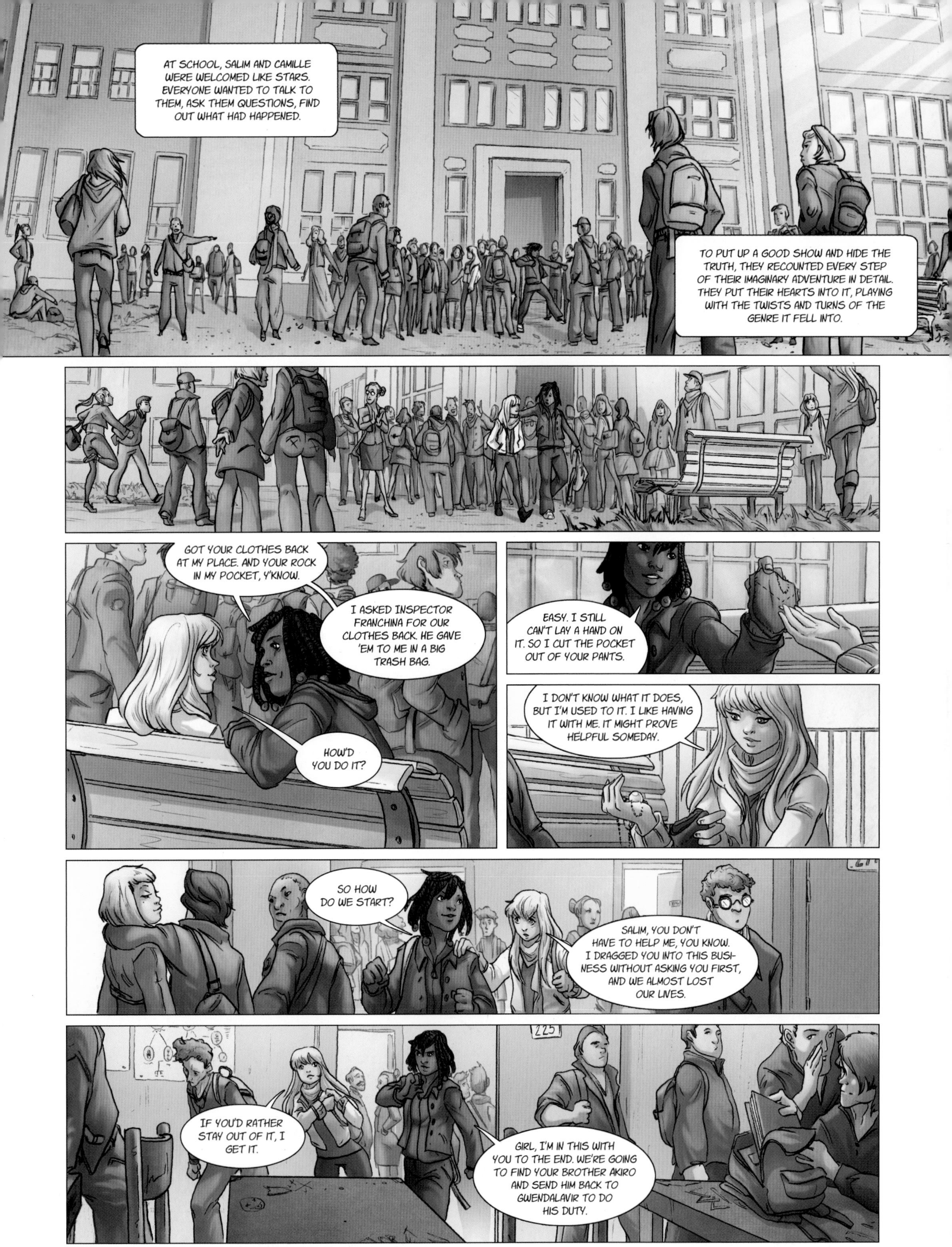
AT SCHOOL, SALIM AND CAMILLE WERE WELCOMED LIKE STARS. EVERYONE WANTED TO TALK TO THEM, ASK THEM QUESTIONS, FIND OUT WHAT HAD HAPPENED.
TO PUT UP A GOOD SHOW AND HIDE THE TRUTH, THEY RECOUNTED EVERY STEP OF THEIR IMAGINARY ADVENTURE IN DETAIL. THEY PUT THEIR HEARTS INTO IT, PLAYING WITH THE TWISTS AND TURNS OF THE GENRE IT FELL INTO.
GOT YOUR CLOTHES BACK AT MY PLACE. AND YOUR ROCK IN MY POCKET, Y'KNOW.
I ASKED INSPECTOR FRANCHINA FOR OUR CLOTHES BACK. HE GAVE 'EM TO ME IN A BIG TRASH BAG.
HOW'D YOU DO IT?
EASY. I STILL CAN'T LAY A HAND ON IT. SO I CUT THE POCKET OUT OF YOUR PANTS.
I DON'T KNOW WHAT IT DOES, BUT I'M USED TO IT. I LIKE HAVING IT WITH ME. IT MIGHT PROVE HELPFUL SOMEDAY.
SO HOW DO WE START?
SALIM, YOU DON'T HAVE TO HELP ME, YOU KNOW. I DRAGGED YOU INTO THIS BUSINESS WITHOUT ASKING YOU FIRST, AND WE ALMOST LOST OUR LIVES.
225
IF YOU'D RATHER STAY OUT OF IT, I GET IT.
GIRL, I'M IN THIS WITH YOU TO THE END. WE'RE GOING TO FIND YOUR BROTHER AKIRO AND SEND HIM BACK TO GWENDALAVIR TO DO HIS DUTY.

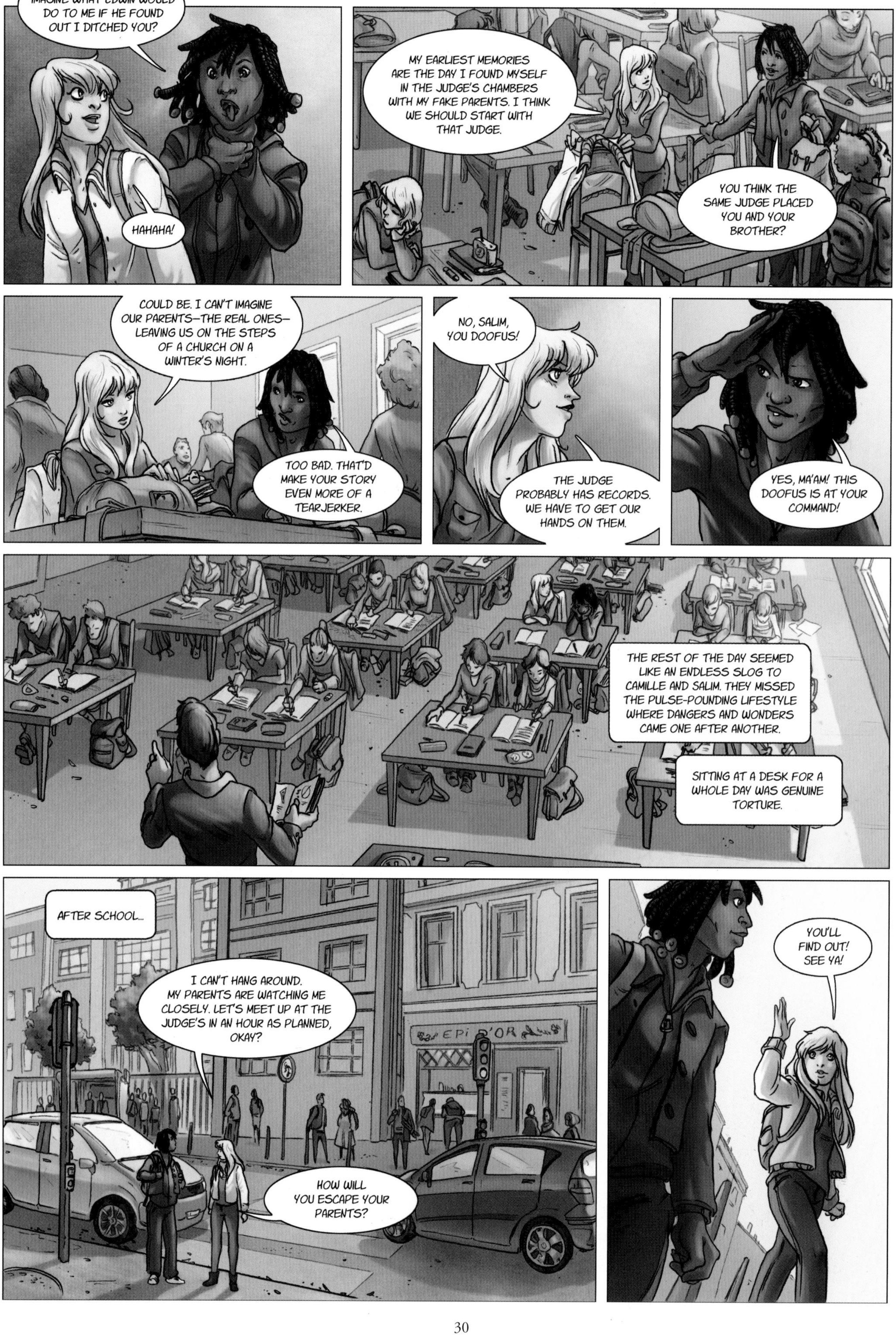
BESIDES, CAN YOU IMAGINE WHAT EDWIN WOULD DO TO ME IF HE FOUND OUT I DITCHED YOU?
HAHAHA!
MY EARLIEST MEMORIES ARE THE DAY I FOUND MYSELF IN THE JUDGE'S CHAMBERS WITH MY FAKE PARENTS. I THINK WE SHOULD START WITH THAT JUDGE.
YOU THINK THE SAME JUDGE PLACED YOU AND YOUR BROTHER?
COULD BE. I CAN'T IMAGINE OUR PARENTS—THE REAL ONES—LEAVING US ON THE STEPS OF A CHURCH ON A WINTER'S NIGHT.
TOO BAD. THAT'D MAKE YOUR STORY EVEN MORE OF A TEARJERKER.
NO, SALIM, YOU DOOFUS!
THE JUDGE PROBABLY HAS RECORDS. WE HAVE TO GET OUR HANDS ON THEM.
YES, MA'AM! THIS DOOFUS IS AT YOUR COMMAND!
THE REST OF THE DAY SEEMED LIKE AN ENDLESS SLOG TO CAMILLE AND SALIM. THEY MISSED THE PULSE-POUNDING LIFESTYLE WHERE DANGERS AND WONDERS CAME ONE AFTER ANOTHER.
SITTING AT A DESK FOR A WHOLE DAY WAS GENUINE TORTURE.
AFTER SCHOOL...
I CAN'T HANG AROUND. MY PARENTS ARE WATCHING ME CLOSELY. LET'S MEET UP AT THE JUDGE'S IN AN HOUR AS PLANNED, OKAY?
EPI D'OR
HOW WILL YOU ESCAPE YOUR PARENTS?
YOU'LL FIND OUT! SEE YA!

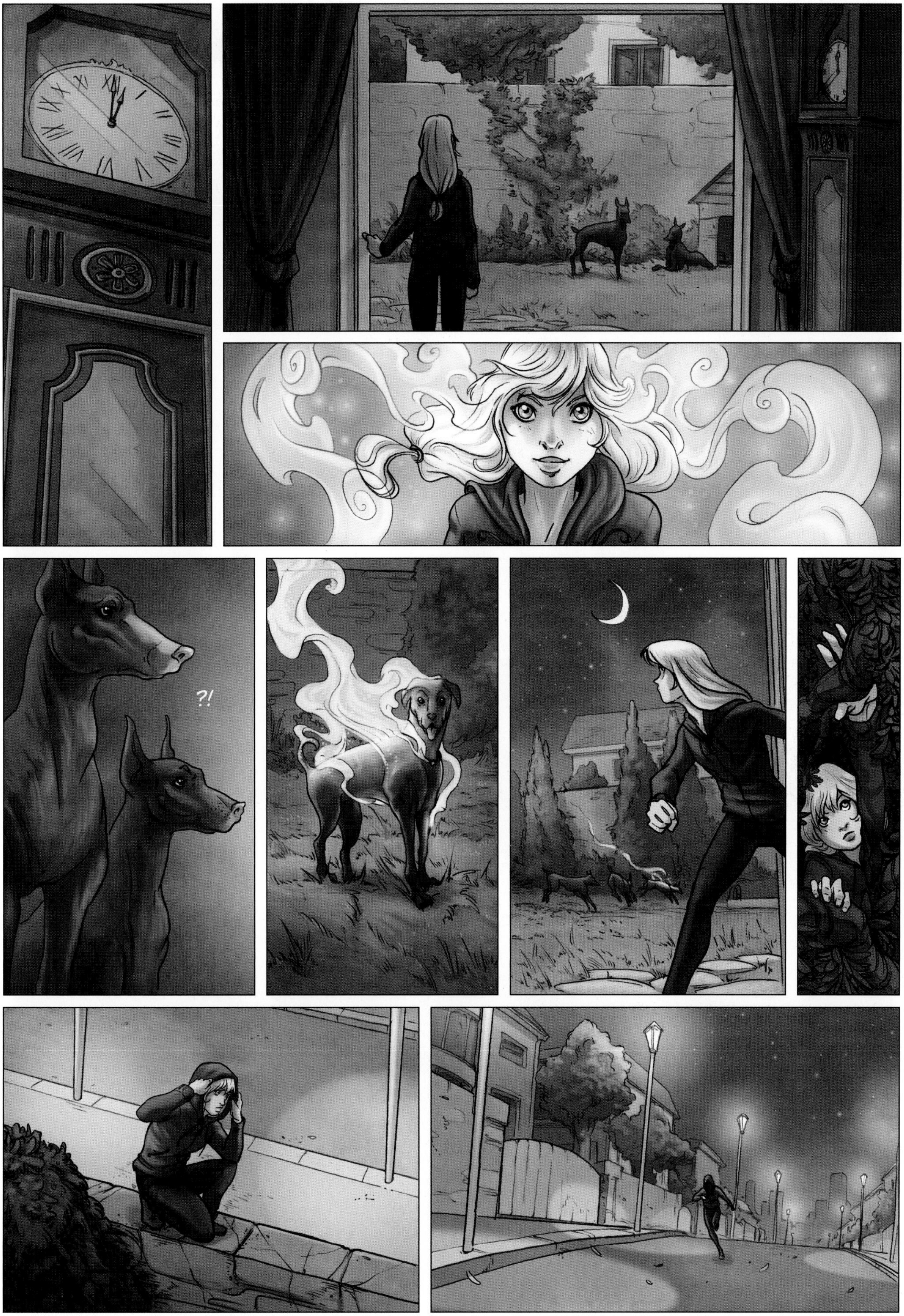
?!

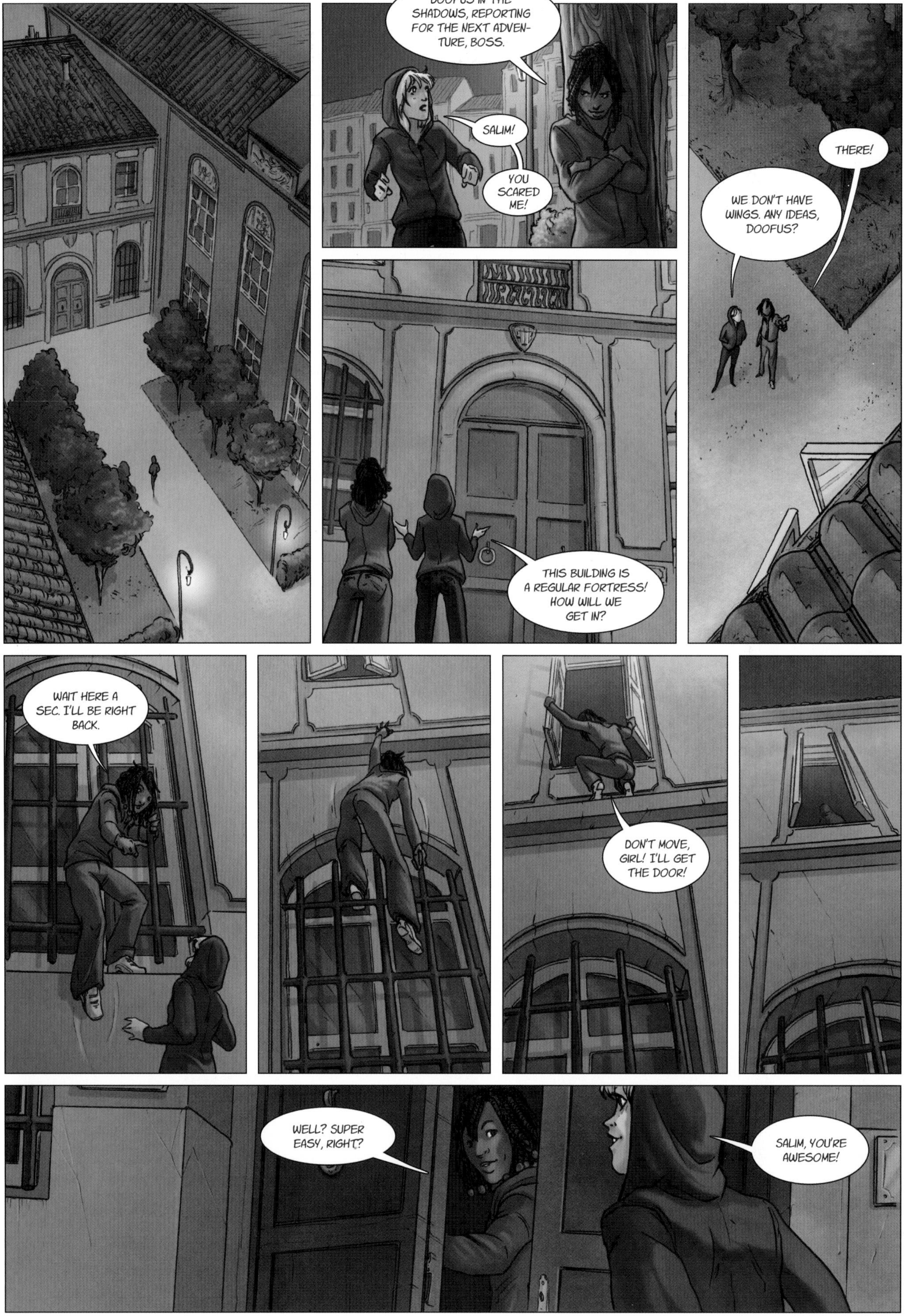
DOOFUS IN THE SHADOWS, REPORTING FOR THE NEXT ADVEN-TURE, BOSS.
SALIM!
YOU SCARED ME!
THIS BUILDING IS A REGULAR FORTRESS! HOW WILL WE GET IN?
WE DON'T HAVE WINGS. ANY IDEAS, DOOFUS?
THERE!
WAIT HERE A SEC. I'LL BE RIGHT BACK.
DON'T MOVE, GIRL! I'LL GET THE DOOR!
WELL? SUPER EASY, RIGHT?
SALIM, YOU'RE AWESOME!

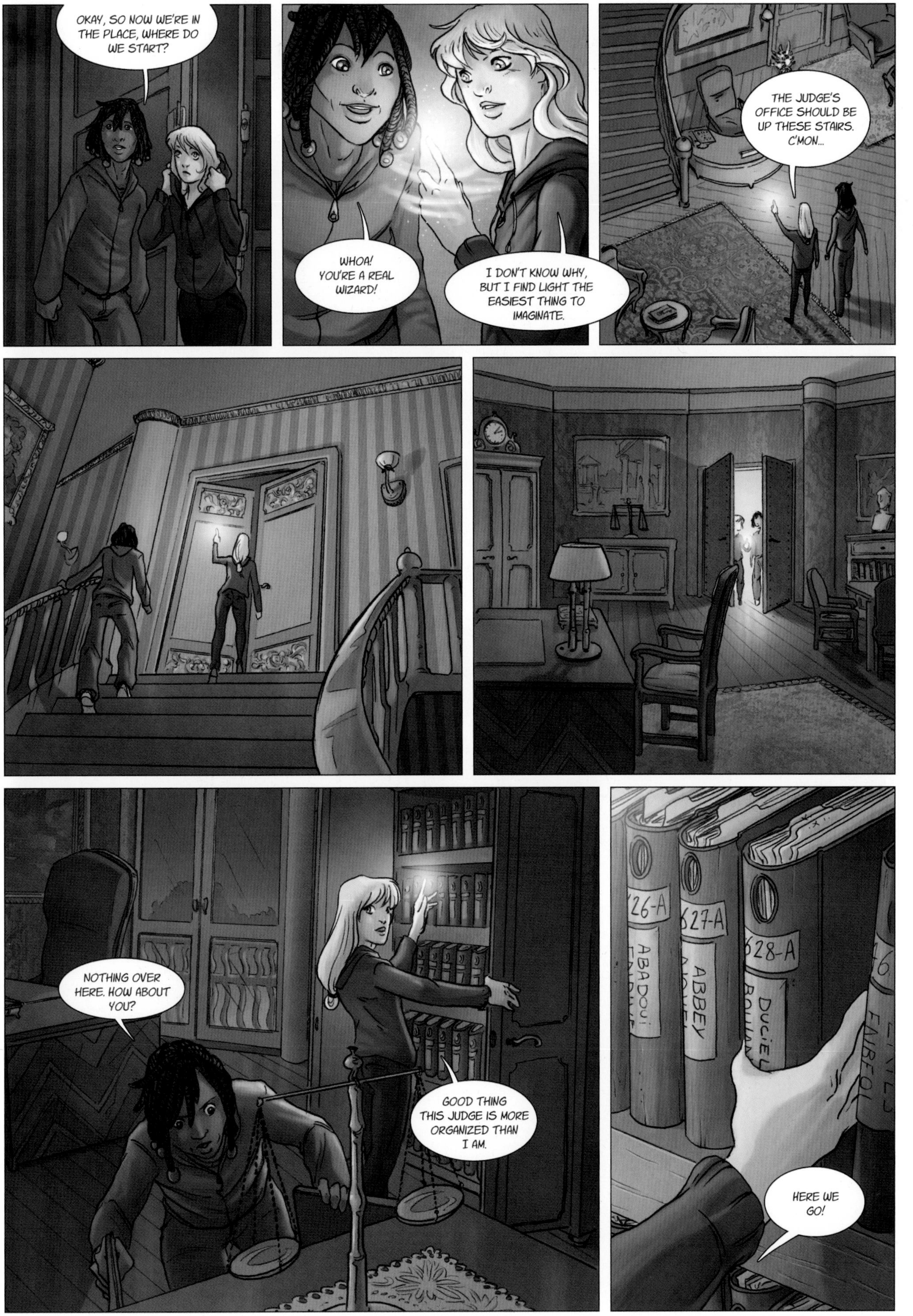
OKAY, SO NOW WE'RE IN THE PLACE, WHERE DO WE START?
WHOA! YOU'RE A REAL WIZARD!
I DON'T KNOW WHY, BUT I FIND LIGHT THE EASIEST THING TO IMAGINATE.
THE JUDGE'S OFFICE SHOULD BE UP THESE STAIRS. C'MON...
NOTHING OVER HERE. HOW ABOUT YOU?
GOOD THING THIS JUDGE IS MORE ORGANIZED THAN I AM.
HERE WE GO!

DUOM WAS RIGHT, GIRL. YOU DO HAVE A BROTHER. IT SAYS SO RIGHT HERE.

HIS NAME IS MATT. HE WAS ADOPTED TWO DAYS BEFORE ME BY A FAMILY NAMED BOULANGER. AND LOOK AT THIS!

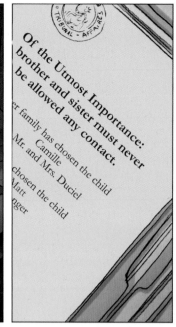

Of the Utmost Importance: brother and sister must never be allowed any contact.

er family has chosen the child
Camille
Mr. and Mrs. Duciel
chosen the child
Matt
nger

IT'S LIKE YOUR REAL PARENTS DELIBERATELY SPLIT YOU UP.

YEAH, I SAW. NOW LET'S GET OUT OF HERE. I'VE GOT EVERY- THING I NEED TO FIND MY BROTHER.

ALL IN ALL, THE OPERATION TOOK LESS THAN AN HOUR.

BUOYED BY THEIR SUCCESSFUL SEARCH, SALIM THOUGHT THEIR QUEST FOR AKIRO WOULD SOON COME TO A TRIUMPHANT END.

FOR HER PART, CAMILLE WAS TURNING OVER IN HER MIND EVERYTHING SHE KNEW ABOUT HER BROTHER.

HE MUST HAVE BEEN EIGHTEEN OR NINETEEN, AND FOR YEARS, HAD LIVED AT 26, RUE DE LA PLAINE. WAS IT POSSIBLE SHE'D CROSSED HIS PATH WITHOUT FEELING A THING? SO MANY DOUBTS, SO MANY QUESTIONS.

HOWEVER, A SINGLE CERTAINTY ENDURED. TOMORROW, SHE WOULD KNOW. TOMORROW, SHE WOULD GO FIND HIM.

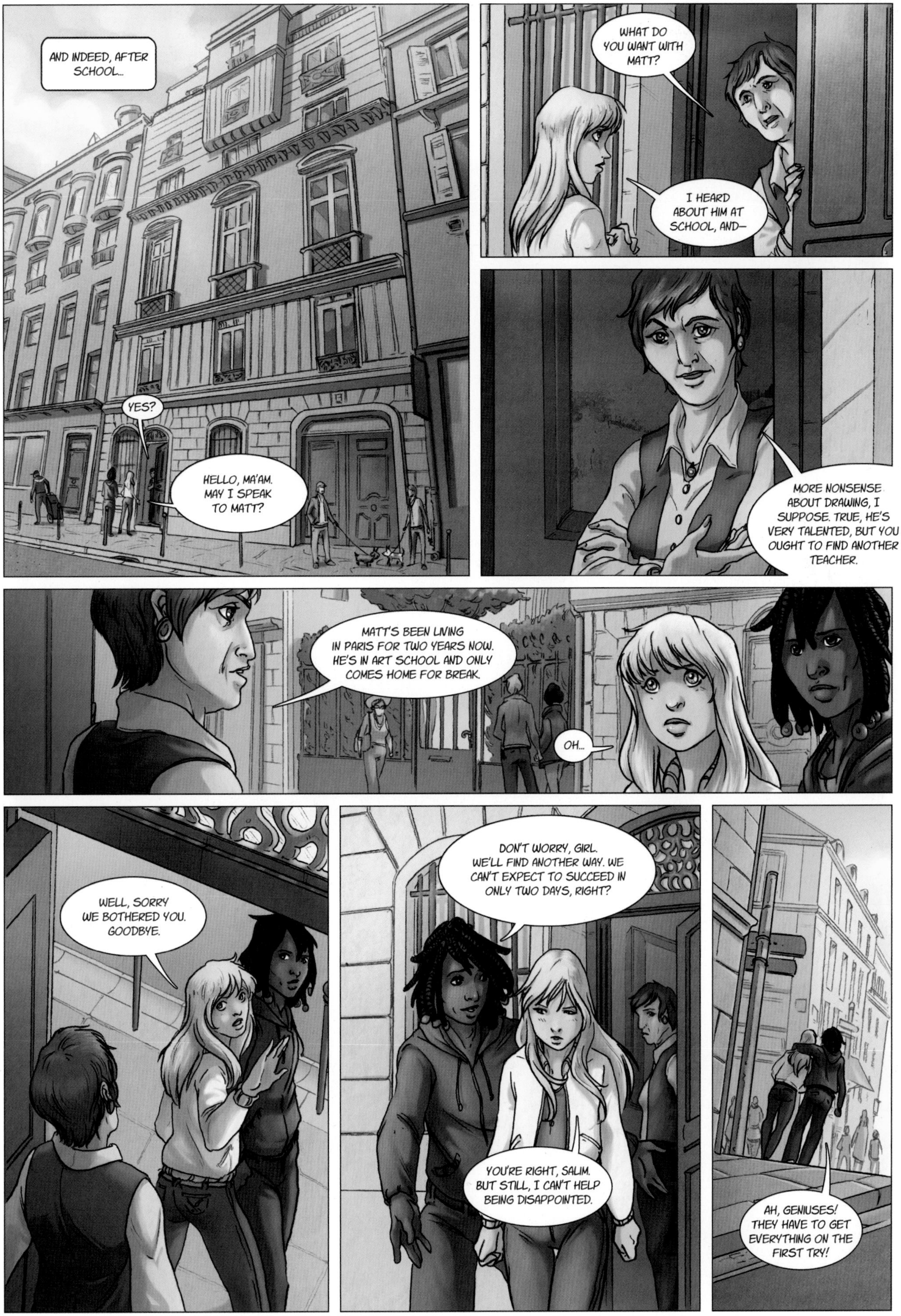
AND INDEED, AFTER SCHOOL...
YES?
HELLO, MA'AM. MAY I SPEAK TO MATT?
WHAT DO YOU WANT WITH MATT?
I HEARD ABOUT HIM AT SCHOOL, AND–
MORE NONSENSE ABOUT DRAWING, I SUPPOSE. TRUE, HE'S VERY TALENTED, BUT YOU OUGHT TO FIND ANOTHER TEACHER.
MATT'S BEEN LIVING IN PARIS FOR TWO YEARS NOW. HE'S IN ART SCHOOL AND ONLY COMES HOME FOR BREAK.
OH...
WELL, SORRY WE BOTHERED YOU. GOODBYE.
DON'T WORRY, GIRL. WE'LL FIND ANOTHER WAY. WE CAN'T EXPECT TO SUCCEED IN ONLY TWO DAYS, RIGHT?
YOU'RE RIGHT, SALIM. BUT STILL, I CAN'T HELP BEING DISAPPOINTED.
AH, GENIUSES! THEY HAVE TO GET EVERYTHING ON THE FIRST TRY!

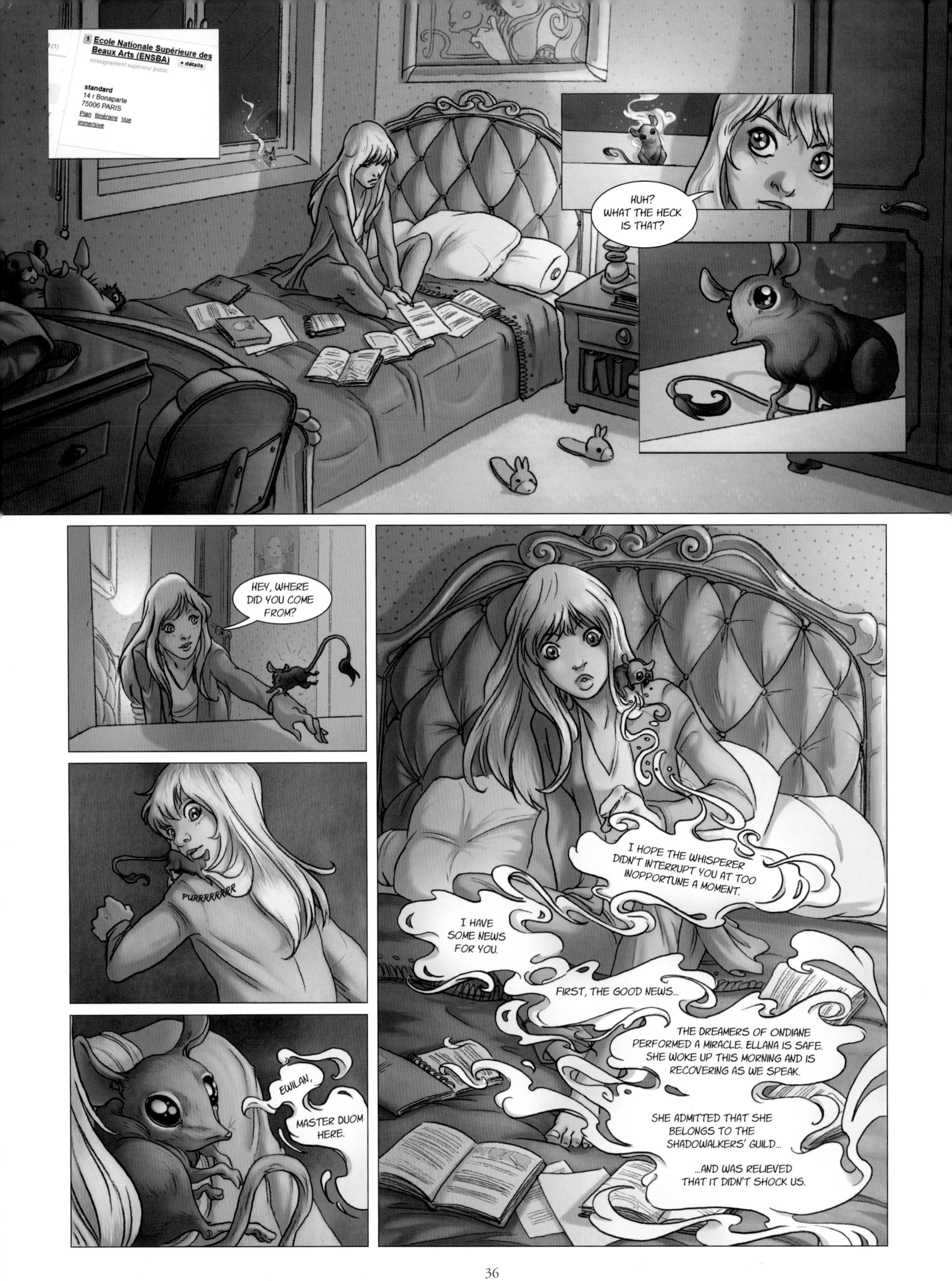
1 Ecole Nationale Supérieure des Beaux Arts (ENSBA)
+ détails
enseignement supérieur public
standard
14 r Bonaparte
75006 PARIS
Plan Itinéraire Vue immersive
HUH? WHAT THE HECK IS THAT?
HEY, WHERE DID YOU COME FROM?
PURRRRRRRR
EWILAN,
MASTER DUOM HERE.
I HOPE THE WHISPERER DIDN'T INTERRUPT YOU AT TOO INOPPORTUNE A MOMENT.
I HAVE SOME NEWS FOR YOU.
FIRST, THE GOOD NEWS...
THE DREAMERS OF ONDIANE PERFORMED A MIRACLE. ELLANA IS SAFE. SHE WOKE UP THIS MORNING AND IS RECOVERING AS WE SPEAK.
SHE ADMITTED THAT SHE BELONGS TO THE SHADOWALKERS' GUILD...
...AND WAS RELIEVED THAT IT DIDN'T SHOCK US.

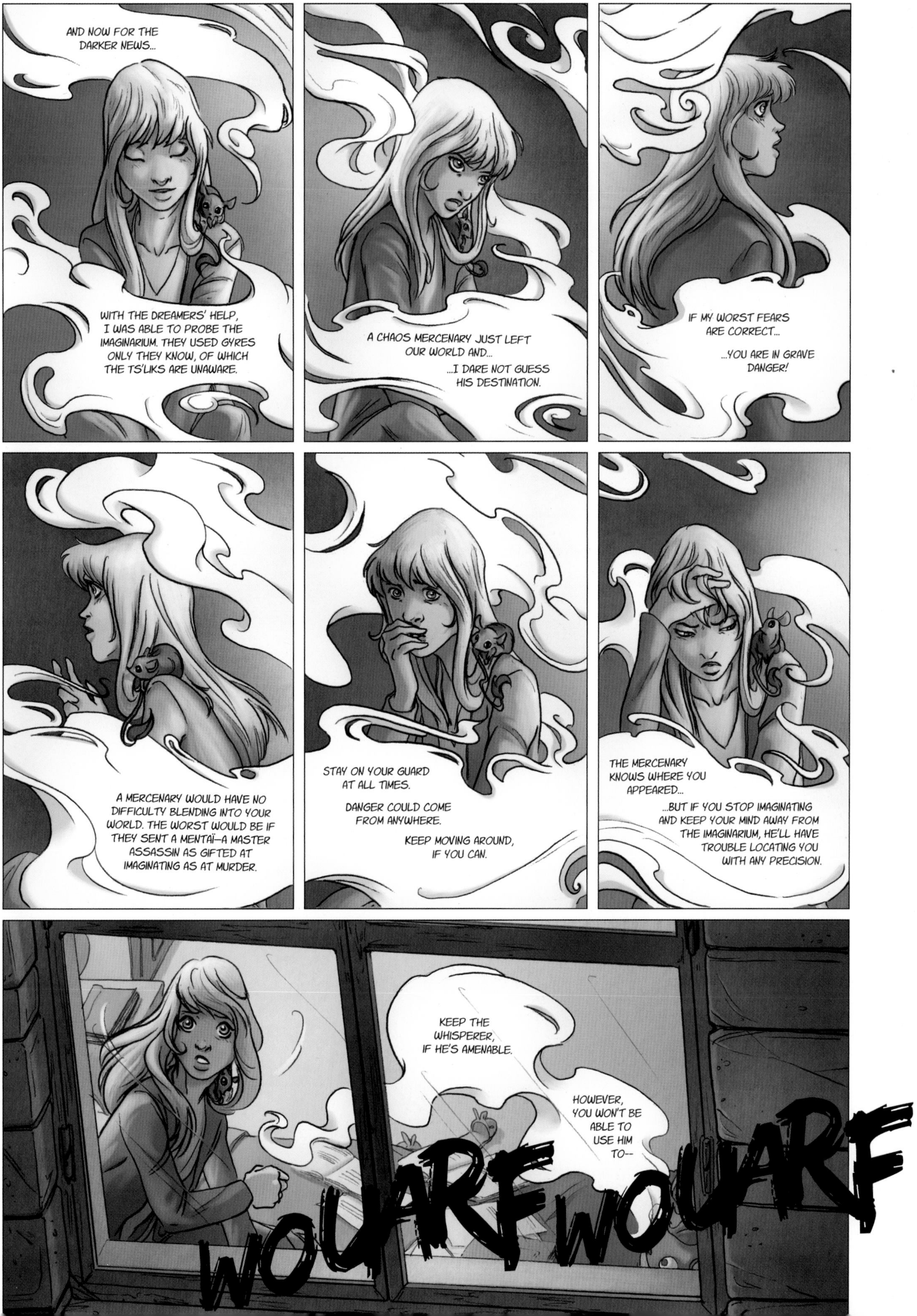
AND NOW FOR THE DARKER NEWS...
WITH THE DREAMERS' HELP, I WAS ABLE TO PROBE THE IMAGINARIUM. THEY USED GYRES ONLY THEY KNOW, OF WHICH THE TS'LIKS ARE UNAWARE.
A CHAOS MERCENARY JUST LEFT OUR WORLD AND...
...I DARE NOT GUESS HIS DESTINATION.
IF MY WORST FEARS ARE CORRECT...
...YOU ARE IN GRAVE DANGER!
A MERCENARY WOULD HAVE NO DIFFICULTY BLENDING INTO YOUR WORLD. THE WORST WOULD BE IF THEY SENT A MENTAÏ—A MASTER ASSASSIN AS GIFTED AT IMAGINATING AS AT MURDER.
STAY ON YOUR GUARD AT ALL TIMES.
DANGER COULD COME FROM ANYWHERE.
KEEP MOVING AROUND, IF YOU CAN.
THE MERCENARY KNOWS WHERE YOU APPEARED...
...BUT IF YOU STOP IMAGINATING AND KEEP YOUR MIND AWAY FROM THE IMAGINARIUM, HE'LL HAVE TROUBLE LOCATING YOU WITH ANY PRECISION.
KEEP THE WHISPERER, IF HE'S AMENABLE.
HOWEVER, YOU WON'T BE ABLE TO USE HIM TO--
WOUARF WOUARF

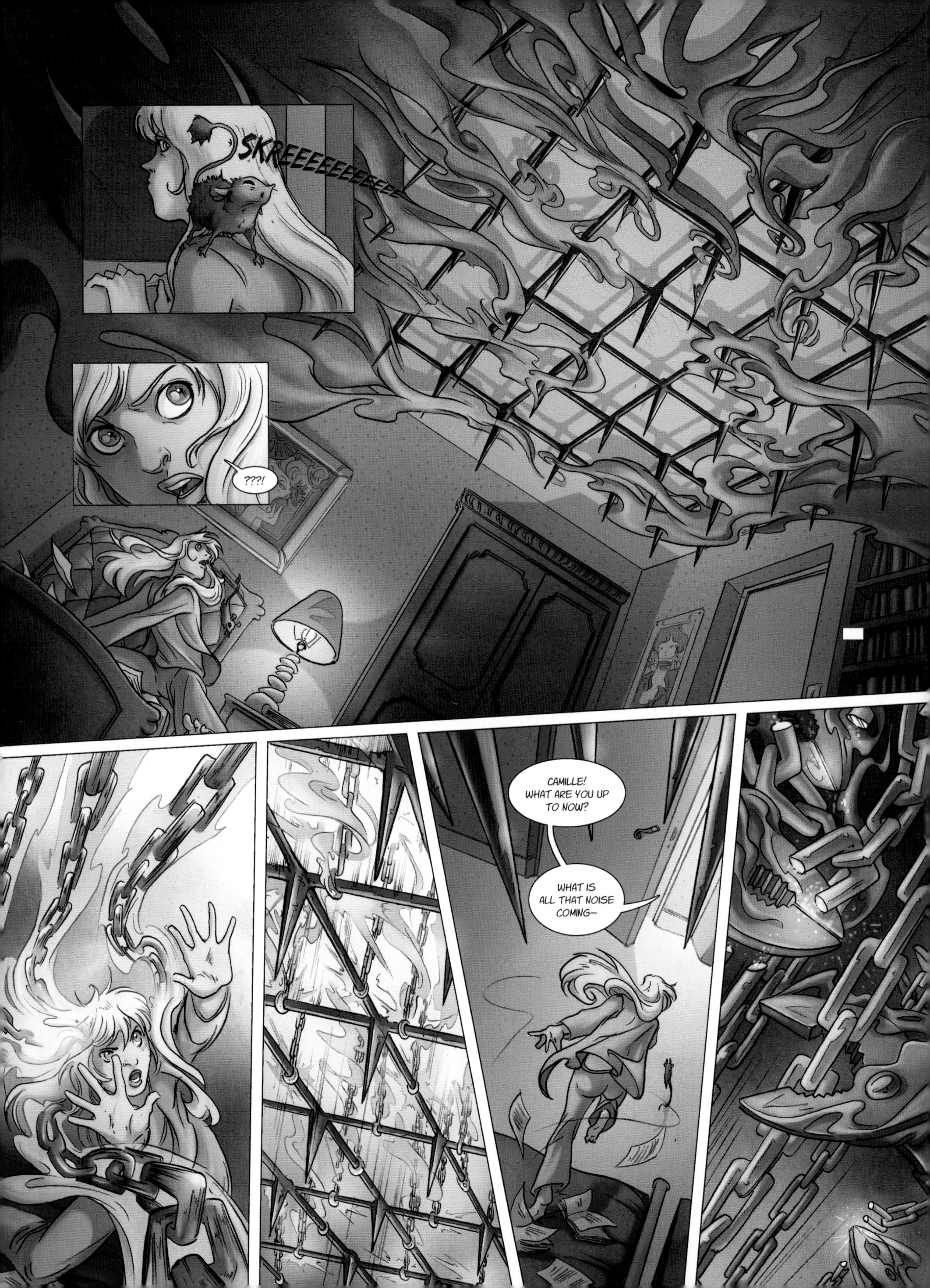
SKREEEEEEEEEEEEE
???!
CAMILLE! WHAT ARE YOU UP TO NOW?
WHAT IS ALL THAT NOISE COMING—

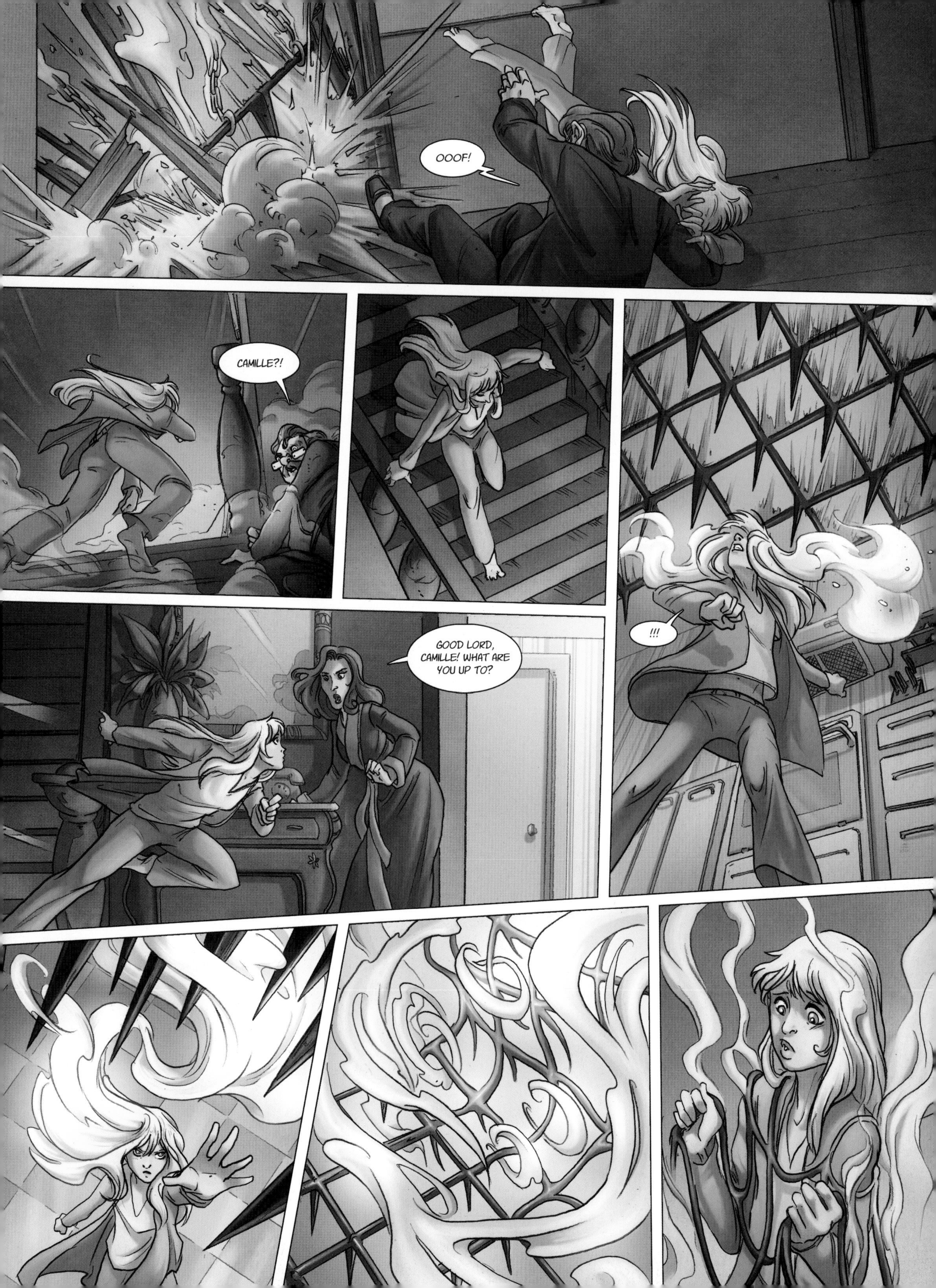
OOOF!
CAMILLE?!
!!!
GOOD LORD, CAMILLE! WHAT ARE YOU UP TO?

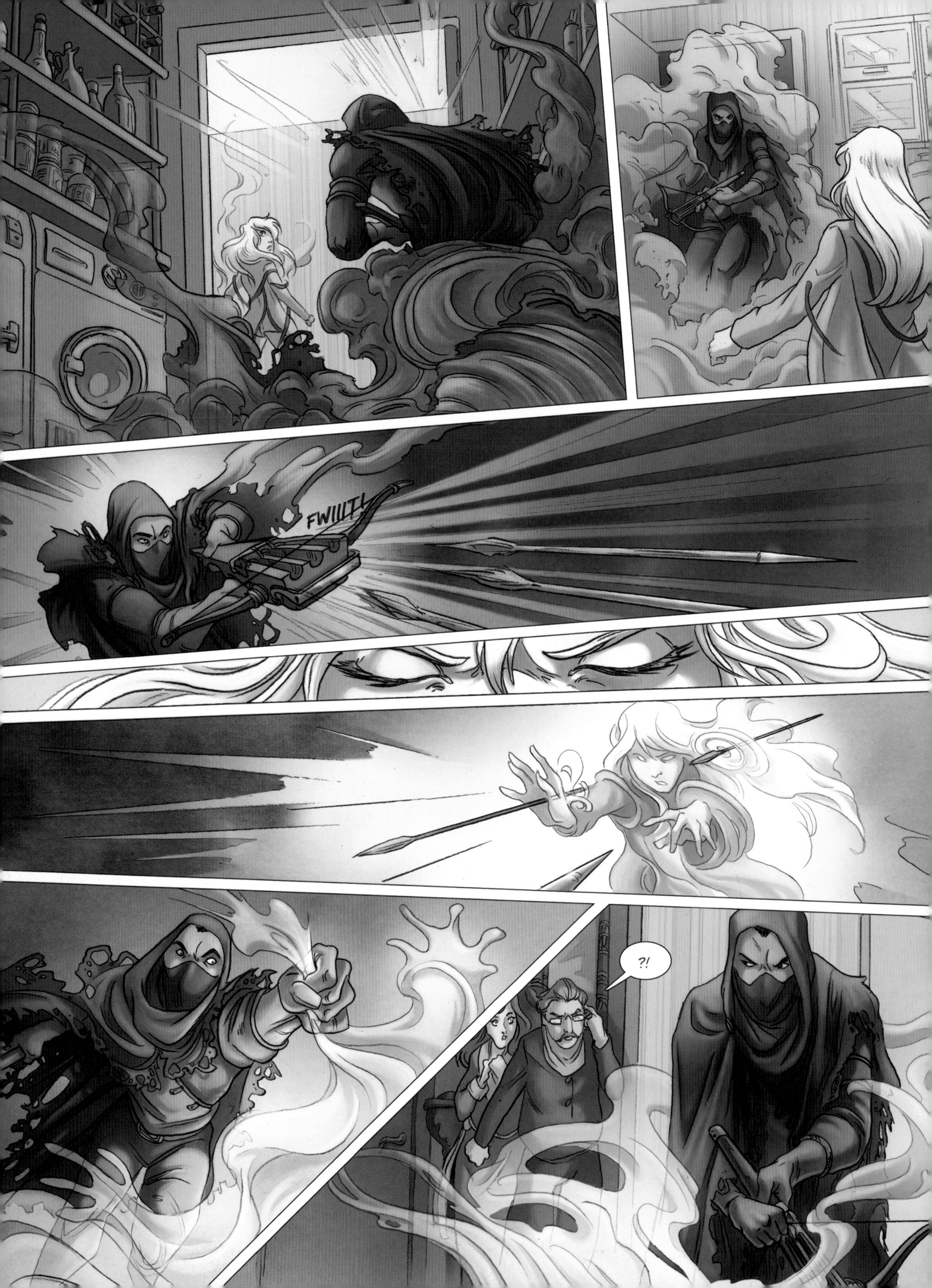
FWIIIT!
?!

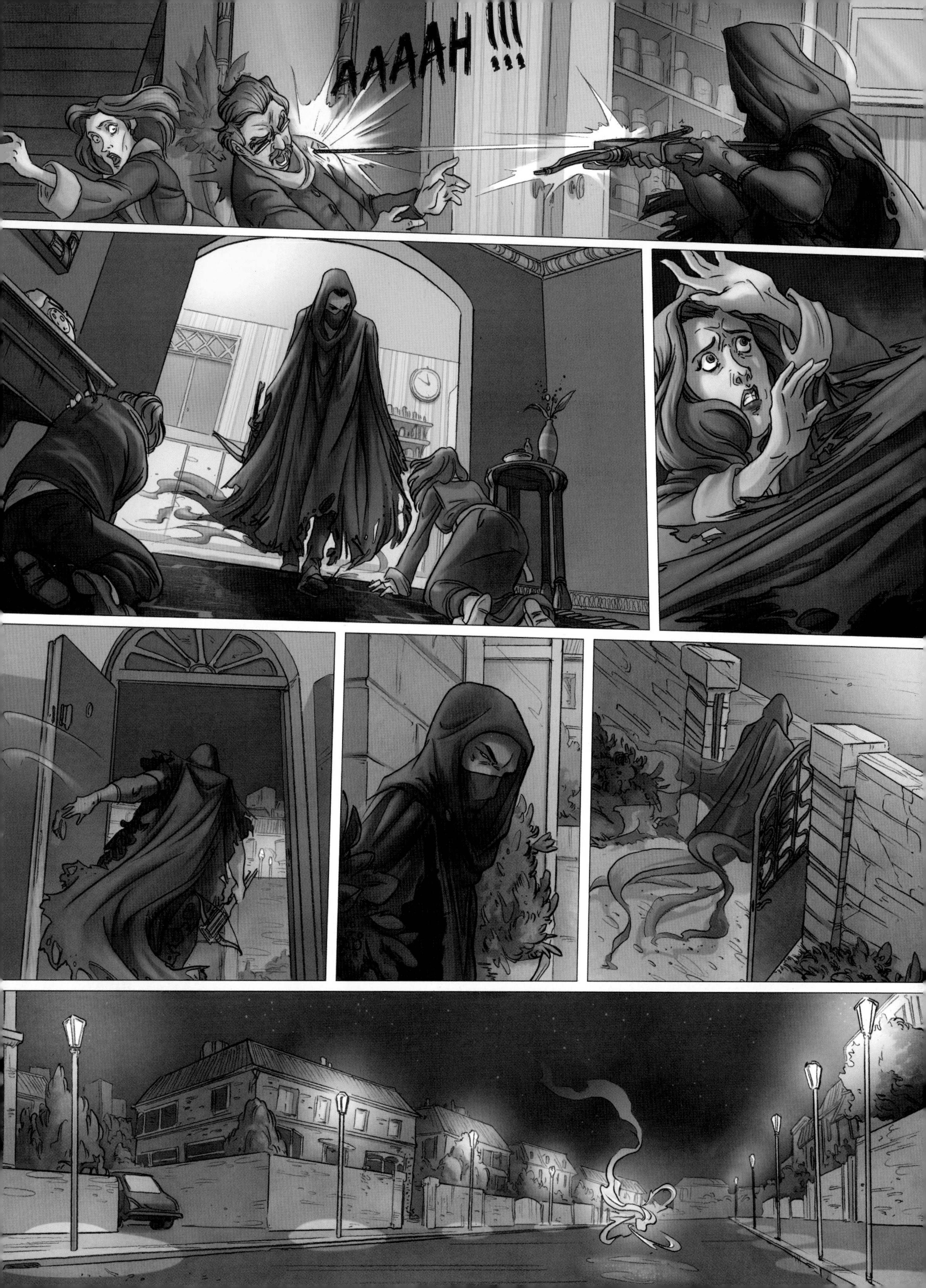
AAAAH !!!

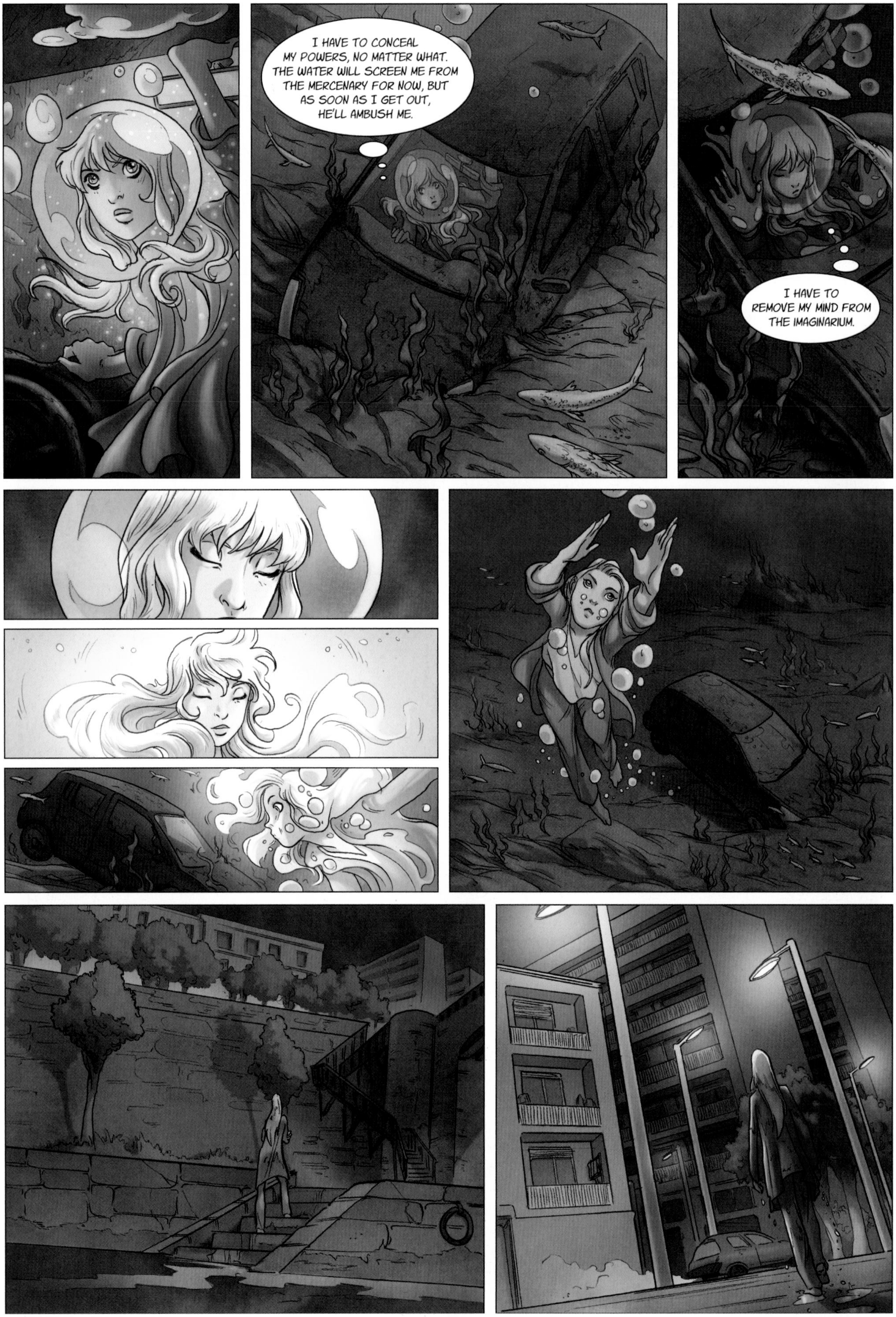
I HAVE TO CONCEAL MY POWERS, NO MATTER WHAT. THE WATER WILL SCREEN ME FROM THE MERCENARY FOR NOW, BUT AS SOON AS I GET OUT, HE'LL AMBUSH ME.
I HAVE TO REMOVE MY MIND FROM THE IMAGINARIUM.

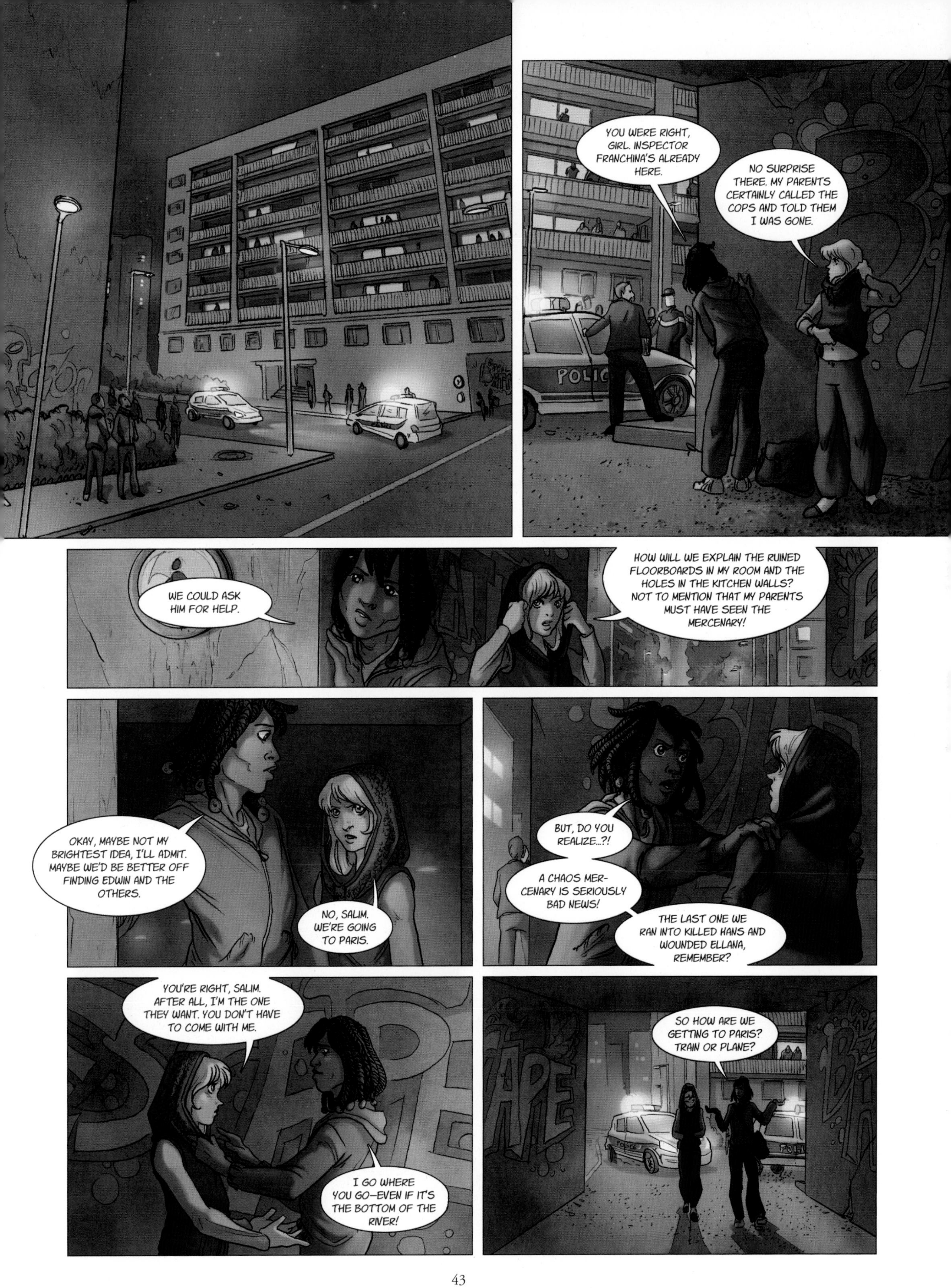
YOU WERE RIGHT, GIRL. INSPECTOR FRANCHINA'S ALREADY HERE.
NO SURPRISE THERE. MY PARENTS CERTAINLY CALLED THE COPS AND TOLD THEM I WAS GONE.
POLIC
WE COULD ASK HIM FOR HELP.
HOW WILL WE EXPLAIN THE RUINED FLOORBOARDS IN MY ROOM AND THE HOLES IN THE KITCHEN WALLS? NOT TO MENTION THAT MY PARENTS MUST HAVE SEEN THE MERCENARY!
OKAY, MAYBE NOT MY BRIGHTEST IDEA, I'LL ADMIT. MAYBE WE'D BE BETTER OFF FINDING EDWIN AND THE OTHERS.
NO, SALIM. WE'RE GOING TO PARIS.
BUT, DO YOU REALIZE...?!
A CHAOS MERCENARY IS SERIOUSLY BAD NEWS!
THE LAST ONE WE RAN INTO KILLED HANS AND WOUNDED ELLANA, REMEMBER?
YOU'RE RIGHT, SALIM. AFTER ALL, I'M THE ONE THEY WANT. YOU DON'T HAVE TO COME WITH ME.
I GO WHERE YOU GO—EVEN IF IT'S THE BOTTOM OF THE RIVER!
SO HOW ARE WE GETTING TO PARIS? TRAIN OR PLANE?

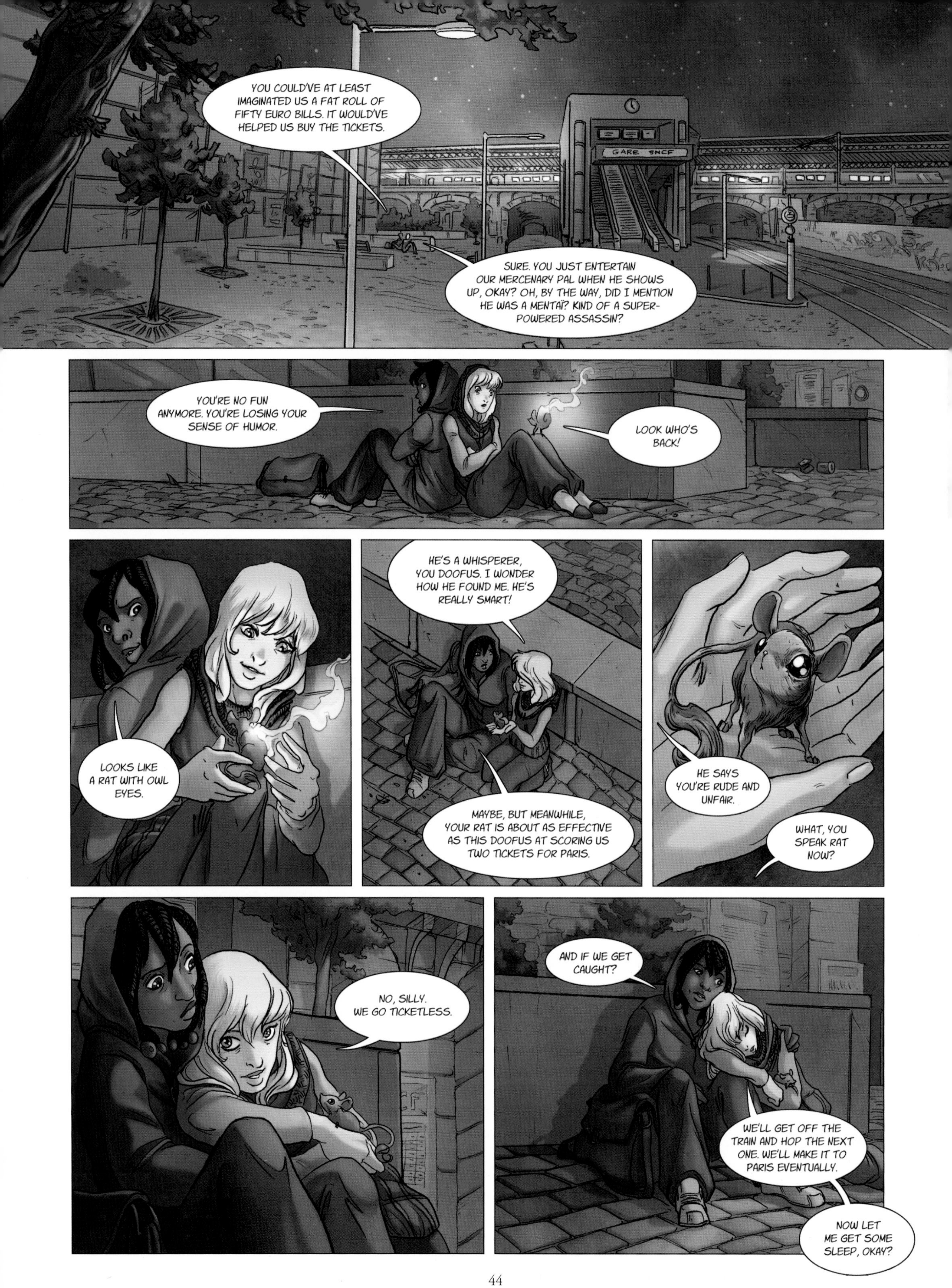

YOU COULD'VE AT LEAST IMAGINATED US A FAT ROLL OF FIFTY EURO BILLS. IT WOULD'VE HELPED US BUY THE TICKETS.
GARE SNCF
SURE. YOU JUST ENTERTAIN OUR MERCENARY PAL WHEN HE SHOWS UP, OKAY? OH, BY THE WAY, DID I MENTION HE WAS A MENTAI? KIND OF A SUPER-POWERED ASSASSIN?
YOU'RE NO FUN ANYMORE. YOU'RE LOSING YOUR SENSE OF HUMOR.
LOOK WHO'S BACK!
LOOKS LIKE A RAT WITH OWL EYES.
HE'S A WHISPERER, YOU DOOFUS. I WONDER HOW HE FOUND ME. HE'S REALLY SMART!
MAYBE, BUT MEANWHILE, YOUR RAT IS ABOUT AS EFFECTIVE AS THIS DOOFUS AT SCORING US TWO TICKETS FOR PARIS.
HE SAYS YOU'RE RUDE AND UNFAIR.
WHAT, YOU SPEAK RAT NOW?
NO, SILLY. WE GO TICKETLESS.
AND IF WE GET CAUGHT?
WE'LL GET OFF THE TRAIN AND HOP THE NEXT ONE. WE'LL MAKE IT TO PARIS EVENTUALLY.
NOW LET ME GET SOME SLEEP, OKAY?

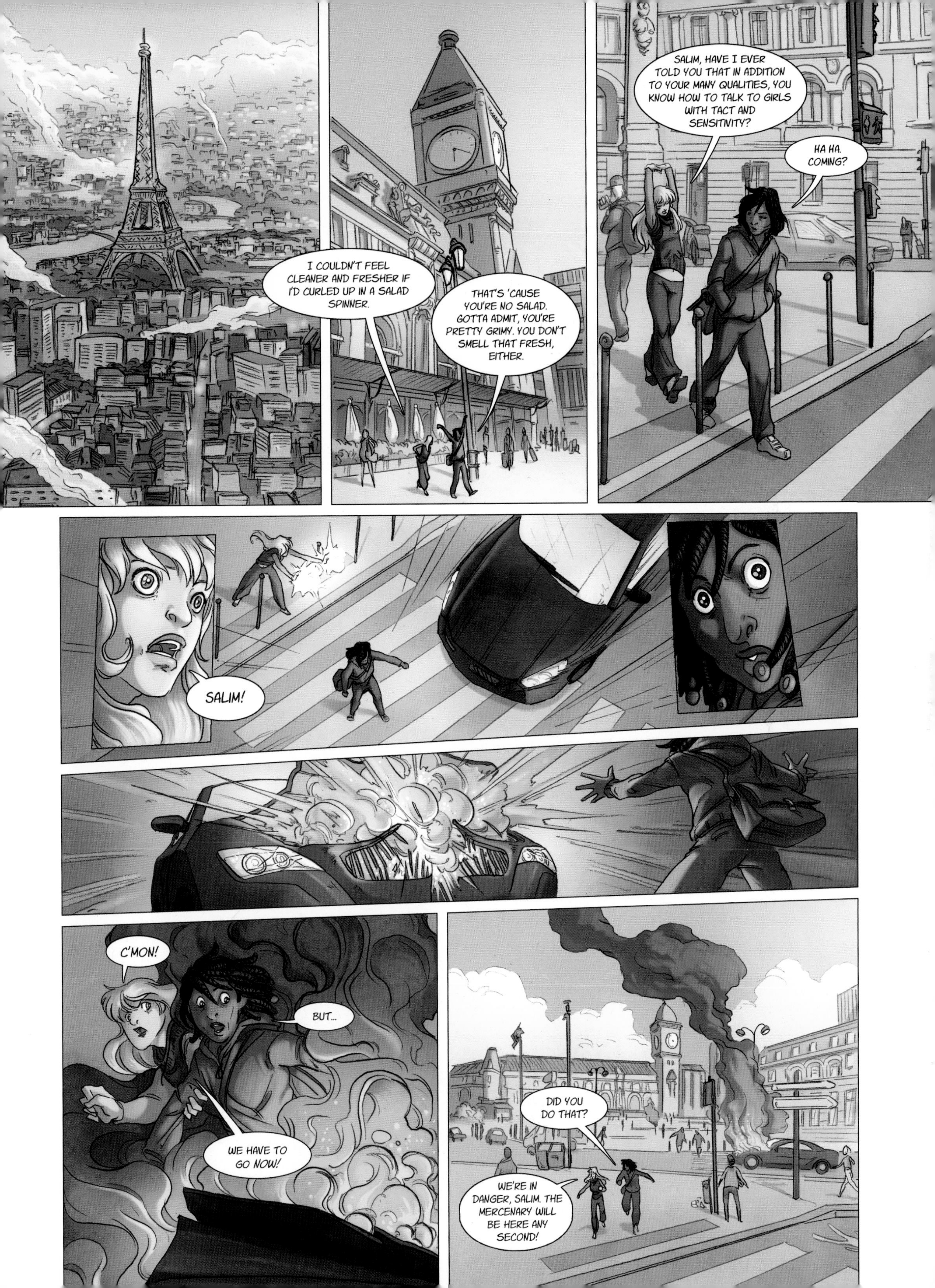
I COULDN'T FEEL CLEANER AND FRESHER IF I'D CURLED UP IN A SALAD SPINNER.
THAT'S 'CAUSE YOU'RE NO SALAD. GOTTA ADMIT, YOU'RE PRETTY GRIMY. YOU DON'T SMELL THAT FRESH, EITHER.
SALIM, HAVE I EVER TOLD YOU THAT IN ADDITION TO YOUR MANY QUALITIES, YOU KNOW HOW TO TALK TO GIRLS WITH TACT AND SENSITIVITY?
HA HA. COMING?
SALIM!
C'MON!
BUT...
WE HAVE TO GO NOW!
DID YOU DO THAT?
WE'RE IN DANGER, SALIM. THE MERCENARY WILL BE HERE ANY SECOND!

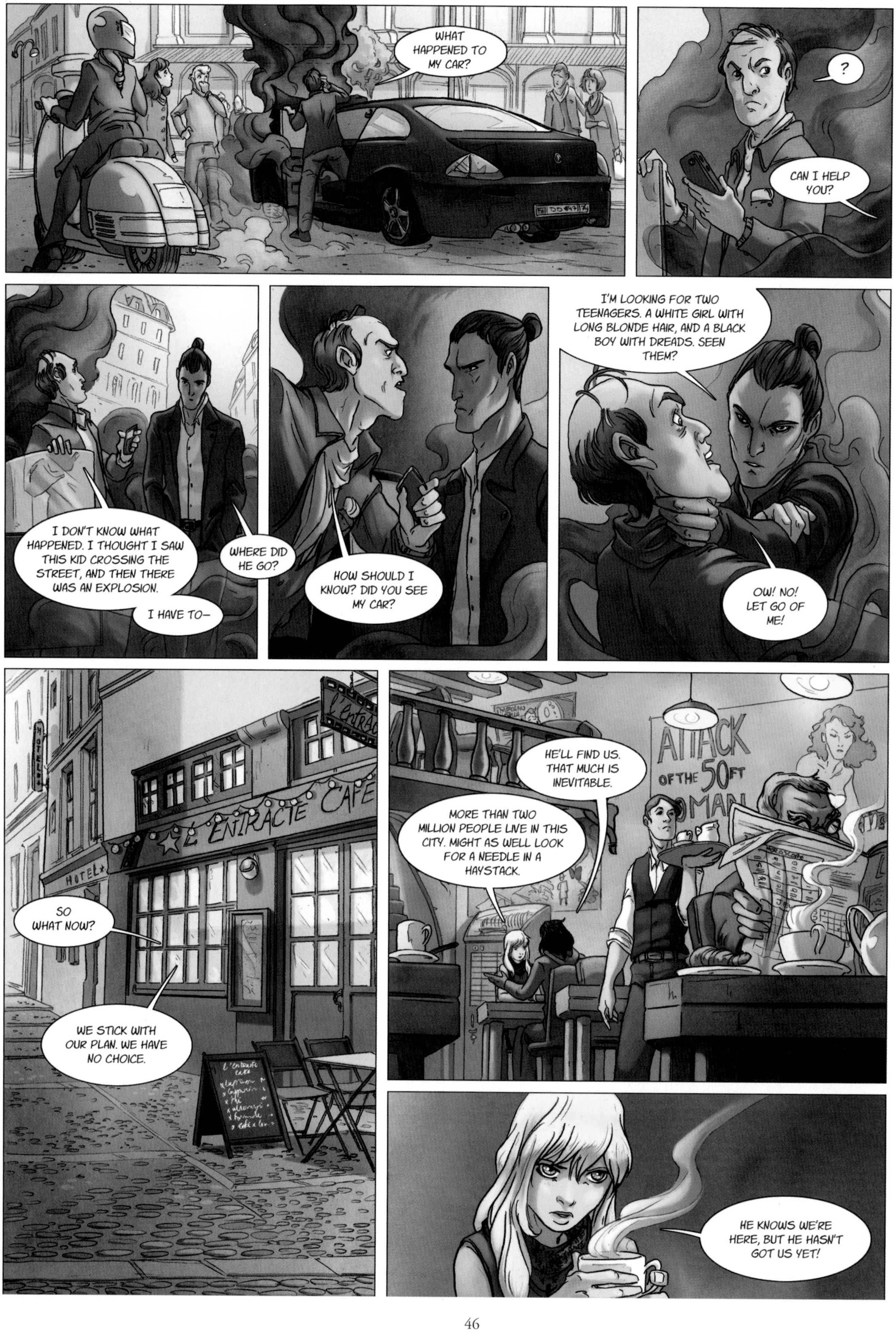
WHAT HAPPENED TO MY CAR?
?
CAN I HELP YOU?
I DON'T KNOW WHAT HAPPENED. I THOUGHT I SAW THIS KID CROSSING THE STREET, AND THEN THERE WAS AN EXPLOSION.
I HAVE TO—
WHERE DID HE GO?
HOW SHOULD I KNOW? DID YOU SEE MY CAR?
I'M LOOKING FOR TWO TEENAGERS. A WHITE GIRL WITH LONG BLONDE HAIR, AND A BLACK BOY WITH DREADS. SEEN THEM?
OW! NO! LET GO OF ME!
L'ENTRACTE CAFÉ
HOTEL
SO WHAT NOW?
WE STICK WITH OUR PLAN. WE HAVE NO CHOICE.
ATTACK OF THE 50FT WOMAN
HE'LL FIND US. THAT MUCH IS INEVITABLE.
MORE THAN TWO MILLION PEOPLE LIVE IN THIS CITY. MIGHT AS WELL LOOK FOR A NEEDLE IN A HAYSTACK.
HE KNOWS WE'RE HERE, BUT HE HASN'T GOT US YET!

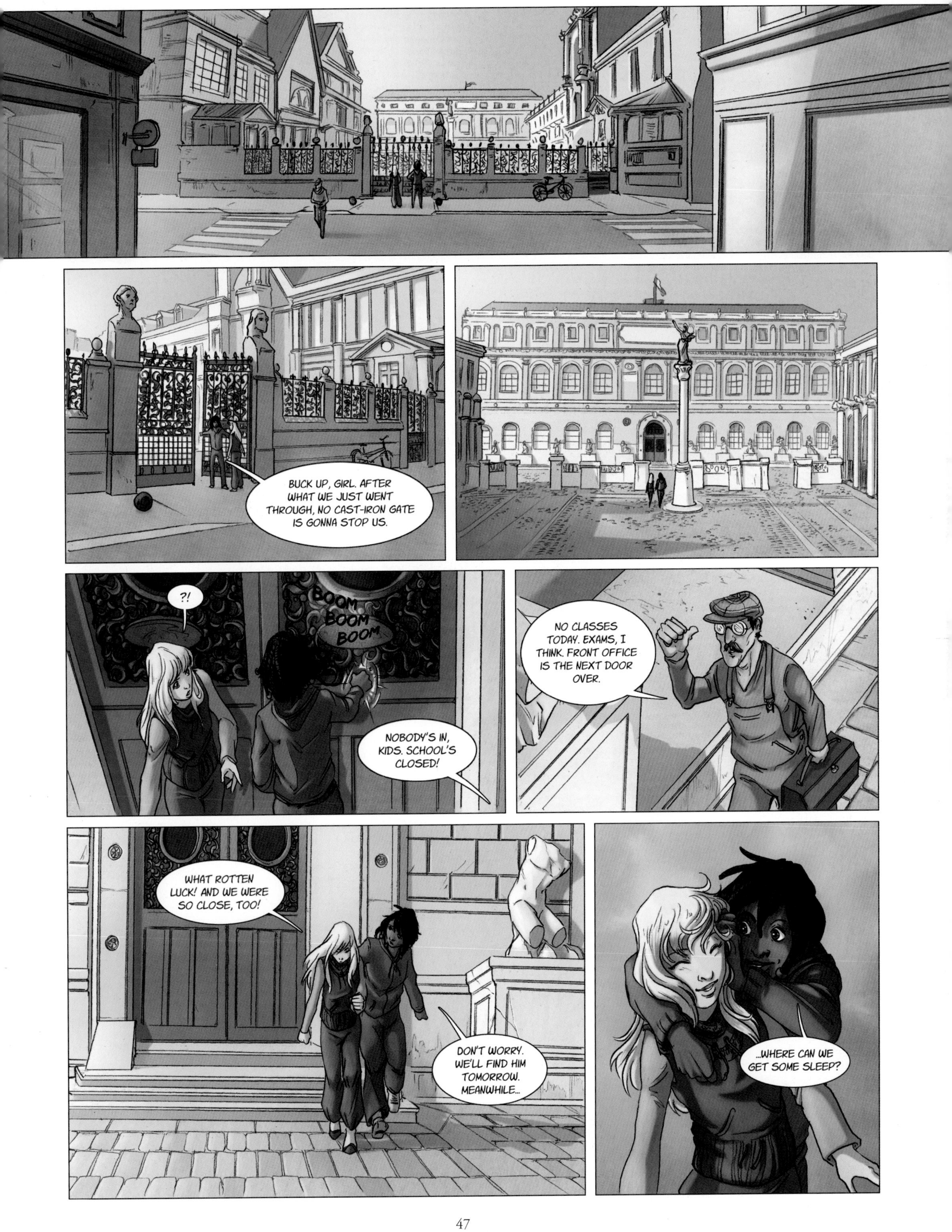
BUCK UP, GIRL. AFTER WHAT WE JUST WENT THROUGH, NO CAST-IRON GATE IS GONNA STOP US.
?!
BOOM BOOM BOOM
NOBODY'S IN, KIDS. SCHOOL'S CLOSED!
NO CLASSES TODAY. EXAMS, I THINK. FRONT OFFICE IS THE NEXT DOOR OVER.
WHAT ROTTEN LUCK! AND WE WERE SO CLOSE, TOO!
DON'T WORRY. WE'LL FIND HIM TOMORROW. MEANWHILE...
...WHERE CAN WE GET SOME SLEEP?

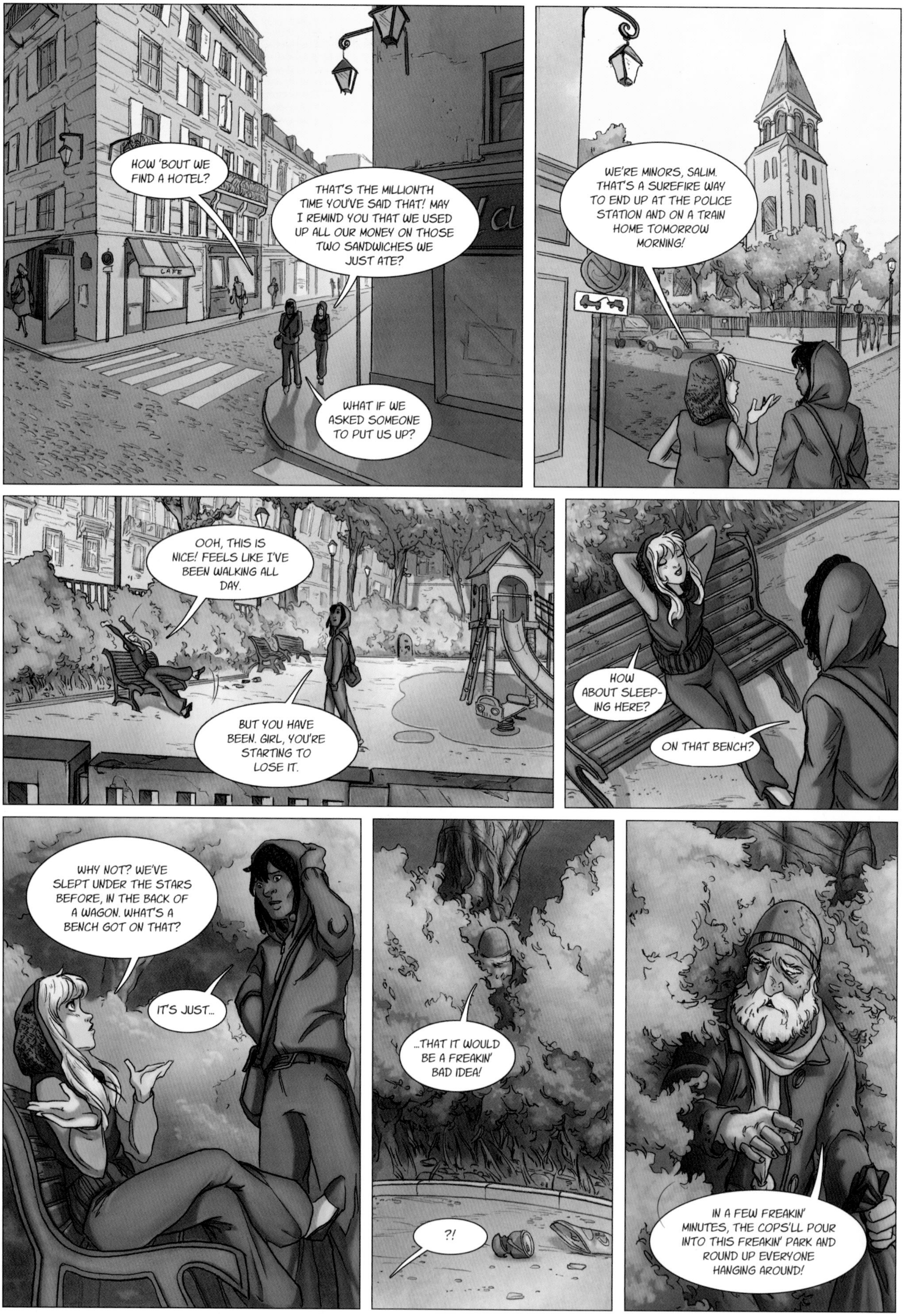
HOW 'BOUT WE FIND A HOTEL?
THAT'S THE MILLIONTH TIME YOU'VE SAID THAT! MAY I REMIND YOU THAT WE USED UP ALL OUR MONEY ON THOSE TWO SANDWICHES WE JUST ATE?
WHAT IF WE ASKED SOMEONE TO PUT US UP?
WE'RE MINORS, SALIM. THAT'S A SUREFIRE WAY TO END UP AT THE POLICE STATION AND ON A TRAIN HOME TOMORROW MORNING!
OOH, THIS IS NICE! FEELS LIKE I'VE BEEN WALKING ALL DAY.
BUT YOU HAVE BEEN. GIRL, YOU'RE STARTING TO LOSE IT.
HOW ABOUT SLEEPING HERE?
ON THAT BENCH?
WHY NOT? WE'VE SLEPT UNDER THE STARS BEFORE, IN THE BACK OF A WAGON. WHAT'S A BENCH GOT ON THAT?
IT'S JUST...
...THAT IT WOULD BE A FREAKIN' BAD IDEA!
?!
IN A FEW FREAKIN' MINUTES, THE COPS'LL POUR INTO THIS FREAKIN' PARK AND ROUND UP EVERYONE HANGING AROUND!

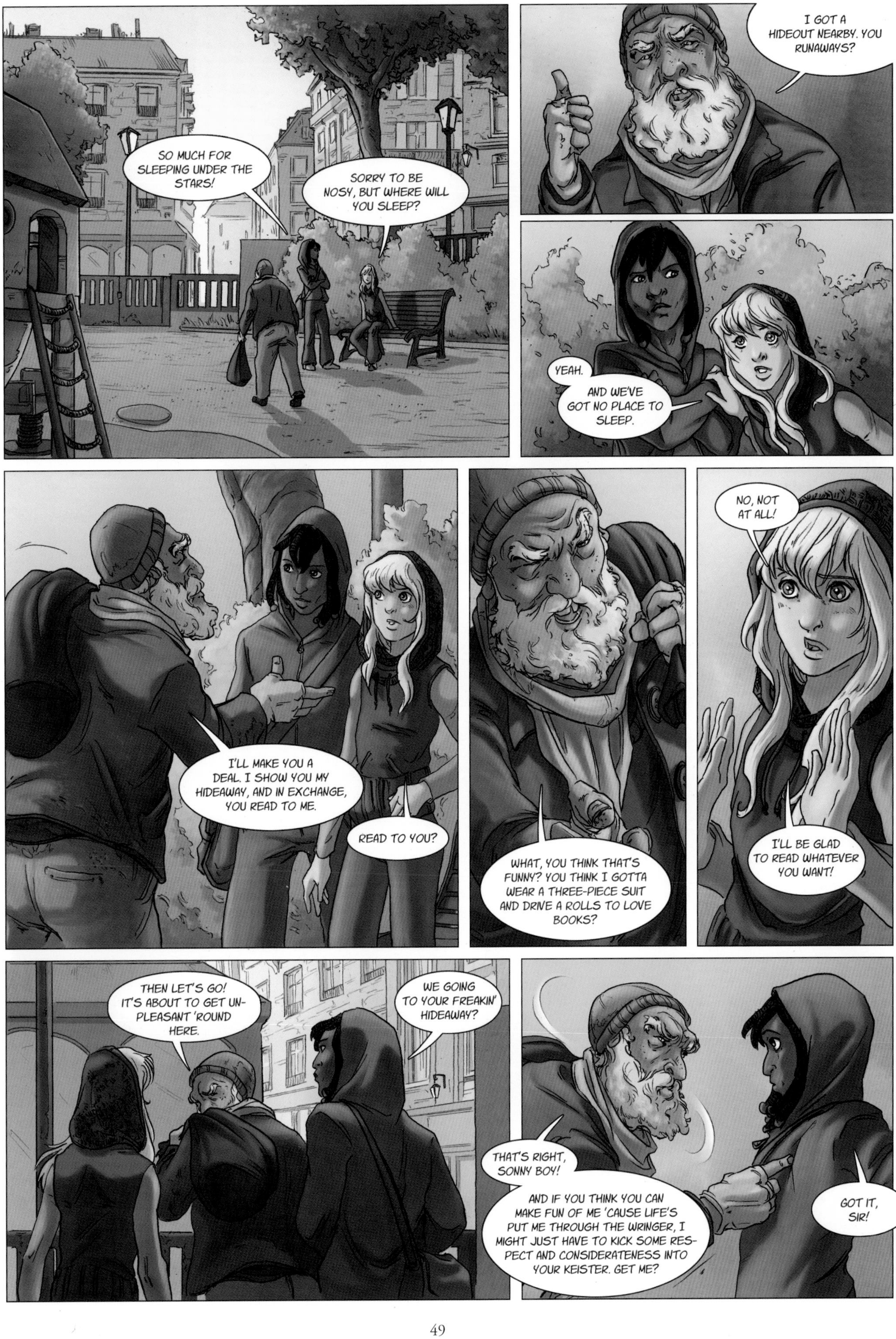
SO MUCH FOR SLEEPING UNDER THE STARS!
SORRY TO BE NOSY, BUT WHERE WILL YOU SLEEP?
I GOT A HIDEOUT NEARBY. YOU RUNAWAYS?
YEAH.
AND WE'VE GOT NO PLACE TO SLEEP.
I'LL MAKE YOU A DEAL. I SHOW YOU MY HIDEAWAY, AND IN EXCHANGE, YOU READ TO ME.
READ TO YOU?
WHAT, YOU THINK THAT'S FUNNY? YOU THINK I GOTTA WEAR A THREE-PIECE SUIT AND DRIVE A ROLLS TO LOVE BOOKS?
NO, NOT AT ALL!
I'LL BE GLAD TO READ WHATEVER YOU WANT!
THEN LET'S GO! IT'S ABOUT TO GET UN-PLEASANT 'ROUND HERE.
WE GOING TO YOUR FREAKIN' HIDEAWAY?
THAT'S RIGHT, SONNY BOY!
AND IF YOU THINK YOU CAN MAKE FUN OF ME 'CAUSE LIFE'S PUT ME THROUGH THE WRINGER, I MIGHT JUST HAVE TO KICK SOME RES-PECT AND CONSIDERATENESS INTO YOUR KEISTER. GET ME?
GOT IT, SIR!

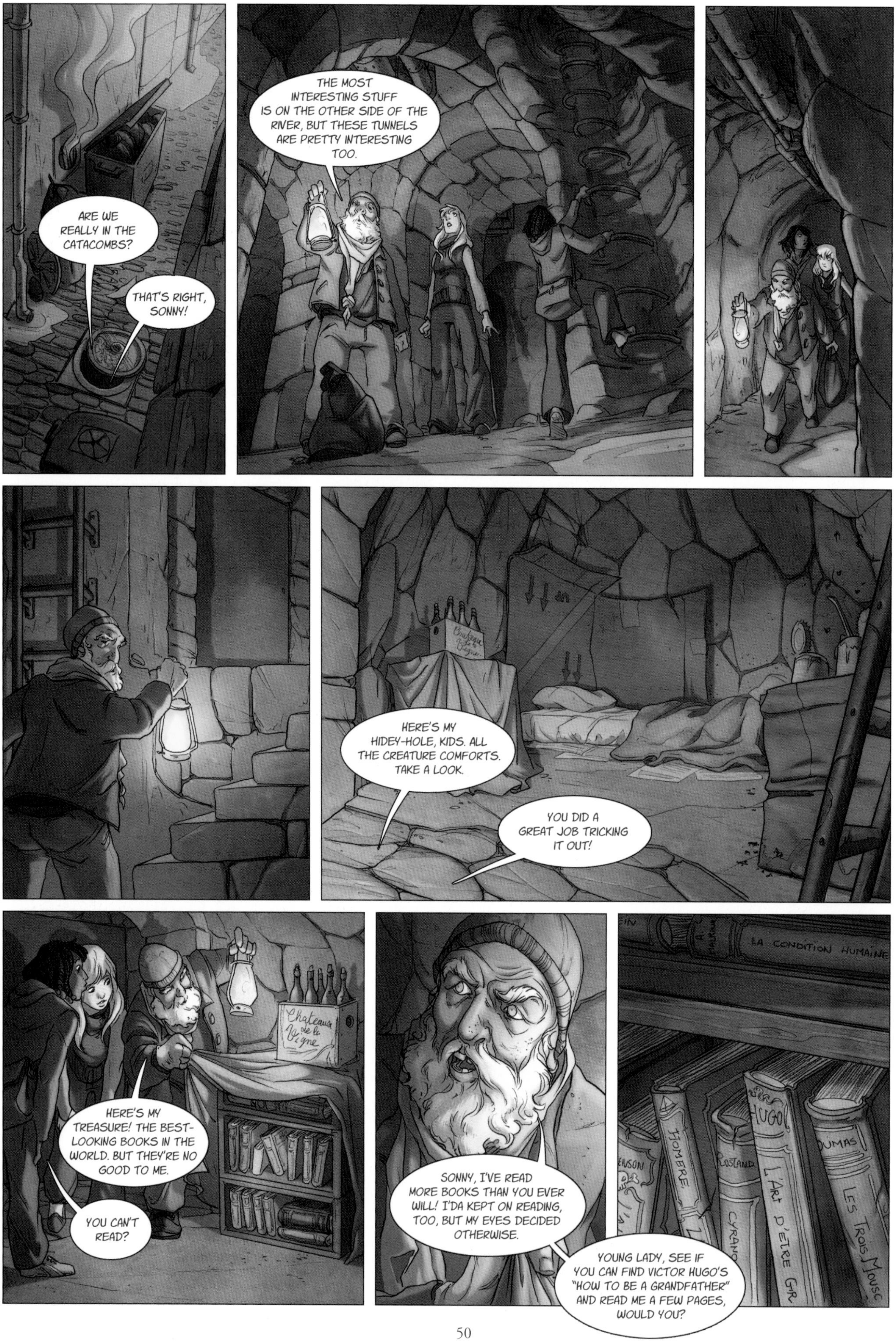

ARE WE REALLY IN THE CATACOMBS?
THAT'S RIGHT, SONNY!
THE MOST INTERESTING STUFF IS ON THE OTHER SIDE OF THE RIVER, BUT THESE TUNNELS ARE PRETTY INTERESTING TOO.
Chateaux de la Vigne
HERE'S MY HIDEY-HOLE, KIDS. ALL THE CREATURE COMFORTS. TAKE A LOOK.
YOU DID A GREAT JOB TRICKING IT OUT!
Chateaux de la Vigne
HERE'S MY TREASURE! THE BEST-LOOKING BOOKS IN THE WORLD. BUT THEY'RE NO GOOD TO ME.
YOU CAN'T READ?
SONNY, I'VE READ MORE BOOKS THAN YOU EVER WILL! I'DA KEPT ON READING, TOO, BUT MY EYES DECIDED OTHERWISE.
YOUNG LADY, SEE IF YOU CAN FIND VICTOR HUGO'S "HOW TO BE A GRANDFATHER" AND READ ME A FEW PAGES, WOULD YOU?
LA CONDITION HUMAINE
HOMERE
HUGO
L'ART D'ÊTRE GR
DUMAS
LES TROIS MOUSC
ROSTAND
CYRANO

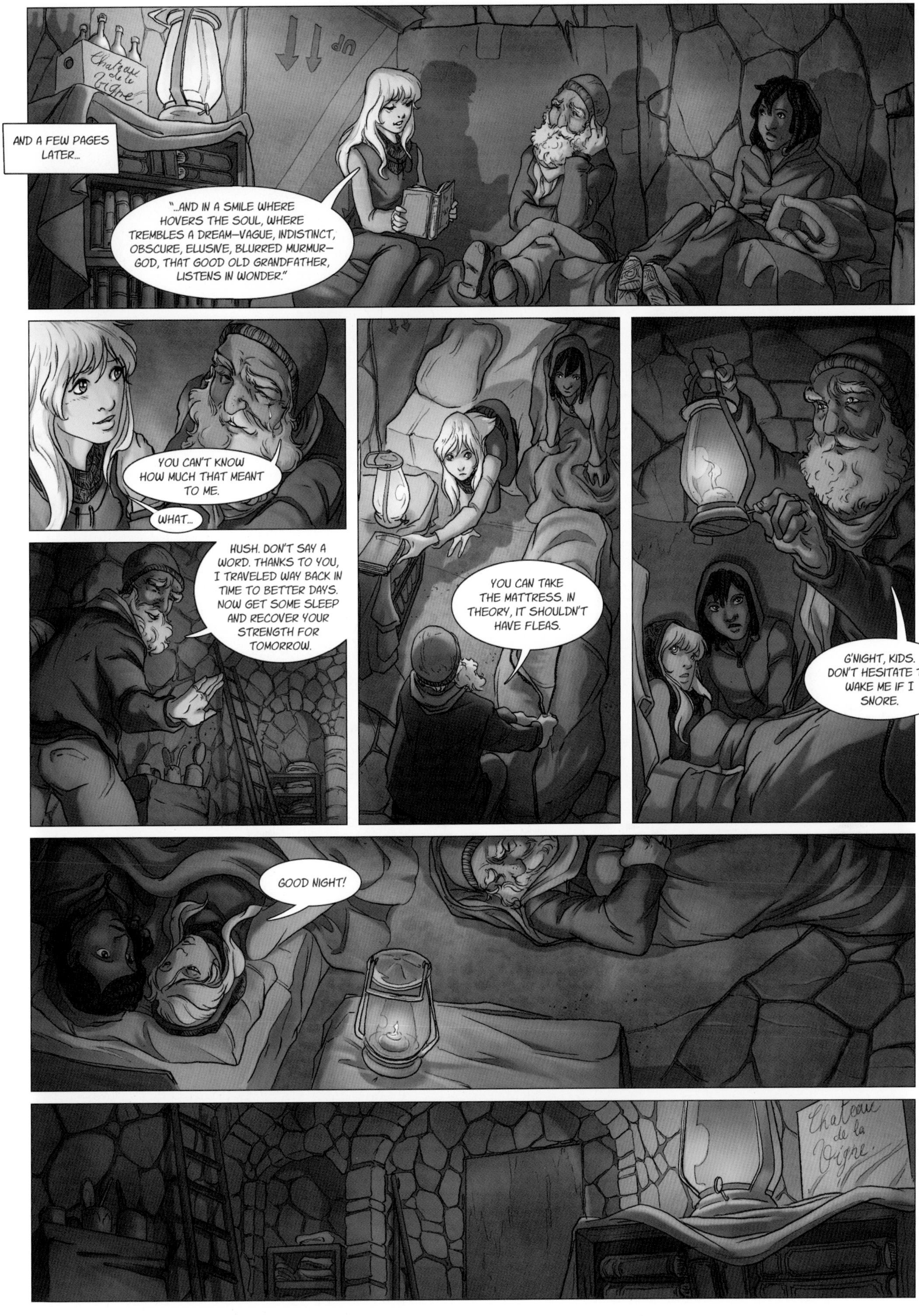
AND A FEW PAGES LATER...
"...AND IN A SMILE WHERE HOVERS THE SOUL, WHERE TREMBLES A DREAM—VAGUE, INDISTINCT, OBSCURE, ELUSIVE, BLURRED MURMUR—GOD, THAT GOOD OLD GRANDFATHER, LISTENS IN WONDER."
YOU CAN'T KNOW HOW MUCH THAT MEANT TO ME.
WHAT...
HUSH. DON'T SAY A WORD. THANKS TO YOU, I TRAVELED WAY BACK IN TIME TO BETTER DAYS. NOW GET SOME SLEEP AND RECOVER YOUR STRENGTH FOR TOMORROW.
YOU CAN TAKE THE MATTRESS. IN THEORY, IT SHOULDN'T HAVE FLEAS.
G'NIGHT, KIDS. DON'T HESITATE TO WAKE ME IF I SNORE.
GOOD NIGHT!

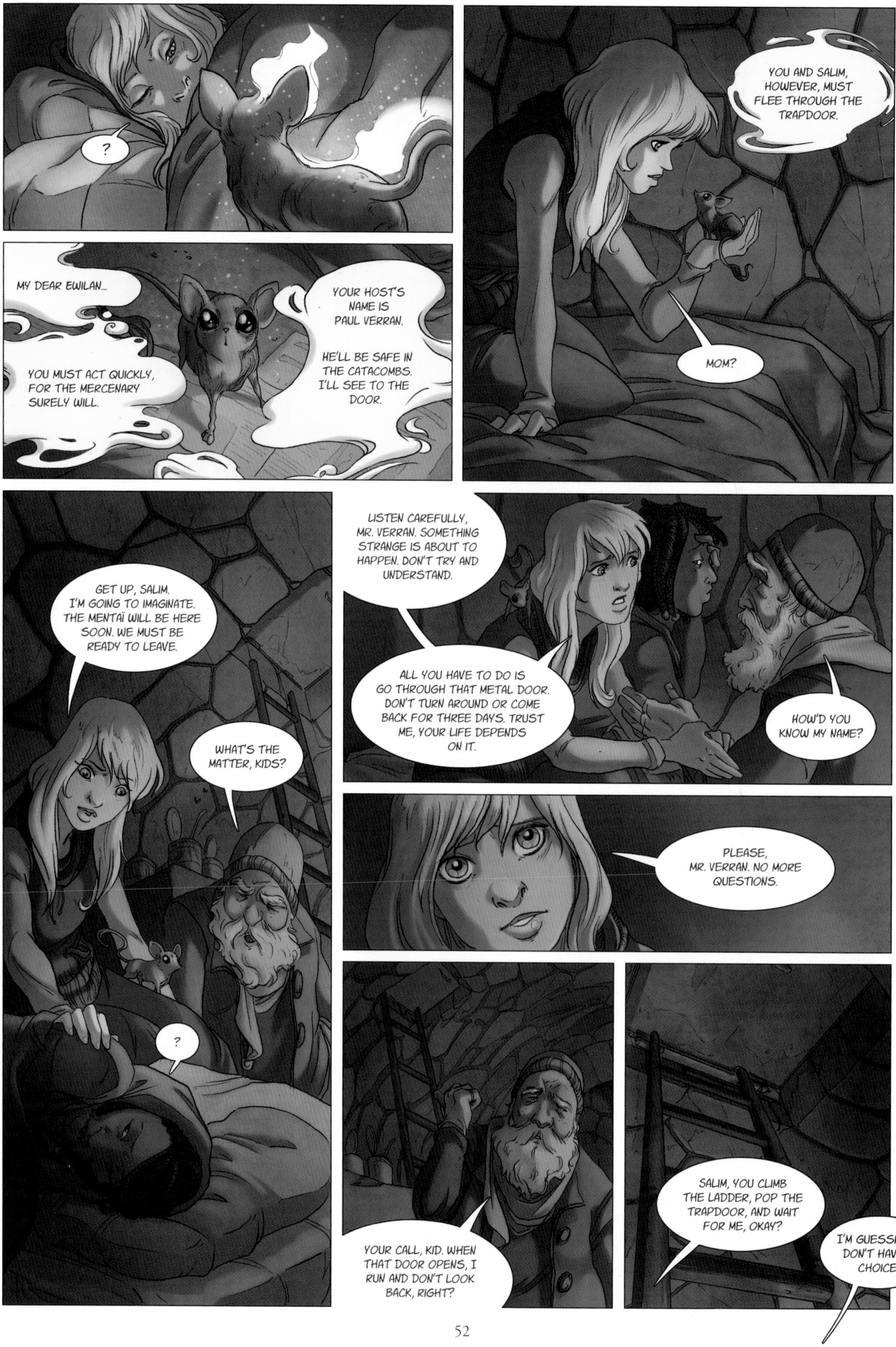

?
YOU AND SALIM, HOWEVER, MUST FLEE THROUGH THE TRAPDOOR.
MY DEAR EWILAN...
YOU MUST ACT QUICKLY, FOR THE MERCENARY SURELY WILL.
YOUR HOST'S NAME IS PAUL VERRAN.
HE'LL BE SAFE IN THE CATACOMBS. I'LL SEE TO THE DOOR.
MOM?
GET UP, SALIM. I'M GOING TO IMAGINATE. THE MENTAÏ WILL BE HERE SOON. WE MUST BE READY TO LEAVE.
WHAT'S THE MATTER, KIDS?
?
LISTEN CAREFULLY, MR. VERRAN. SOMETHING STRANGE IS ABOUT TO HAPPEN. DON'T TRY AND UNDERSTAND.
ALL YOU HAVE TO DO IS GO THROUGH THAT METAL DOOR. DON'T TURN AROUND OR COME BACK FOR THREE DAYS. TRUST ME, YOUR LIFE DEPENDS ON IT.
HOW'D YOU KNOW MY NAME?
PLEASE, MR. VERRAN. NO MORE QUESTIONS.
YOUR CALL, KID. WHEN THAT DOOR OPENS, I RUN AND DON'T LOOK BACK, RIGHT?
SALIM, YOU CLIMB THE LADDER, POP THE TRAPDOOR, AND WAIT FOR ME, OKAY?
I'M GUESSING I DON'T HAVE A CHOICE.

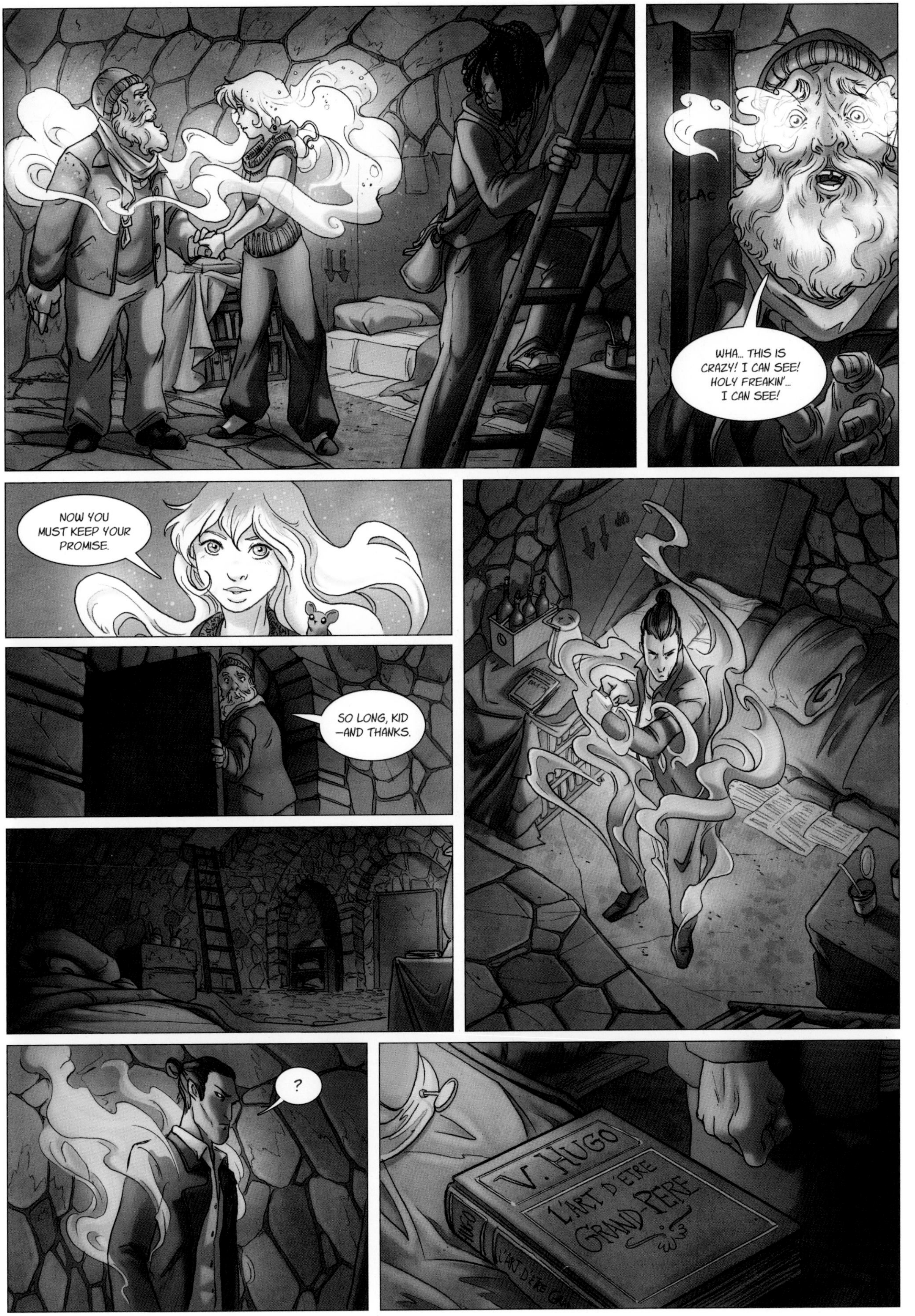
CLAC
WHA... THIS IS CRAZY! I CAN SEE! HOLY FREAKIN'... I CAN SEE!
NOW YOU MUST KEEP YOUR PROMISE.
SO LONG, KID —AND THANKS.
?
V. HUGO
L'ART D'ETRE GRAND-PERE

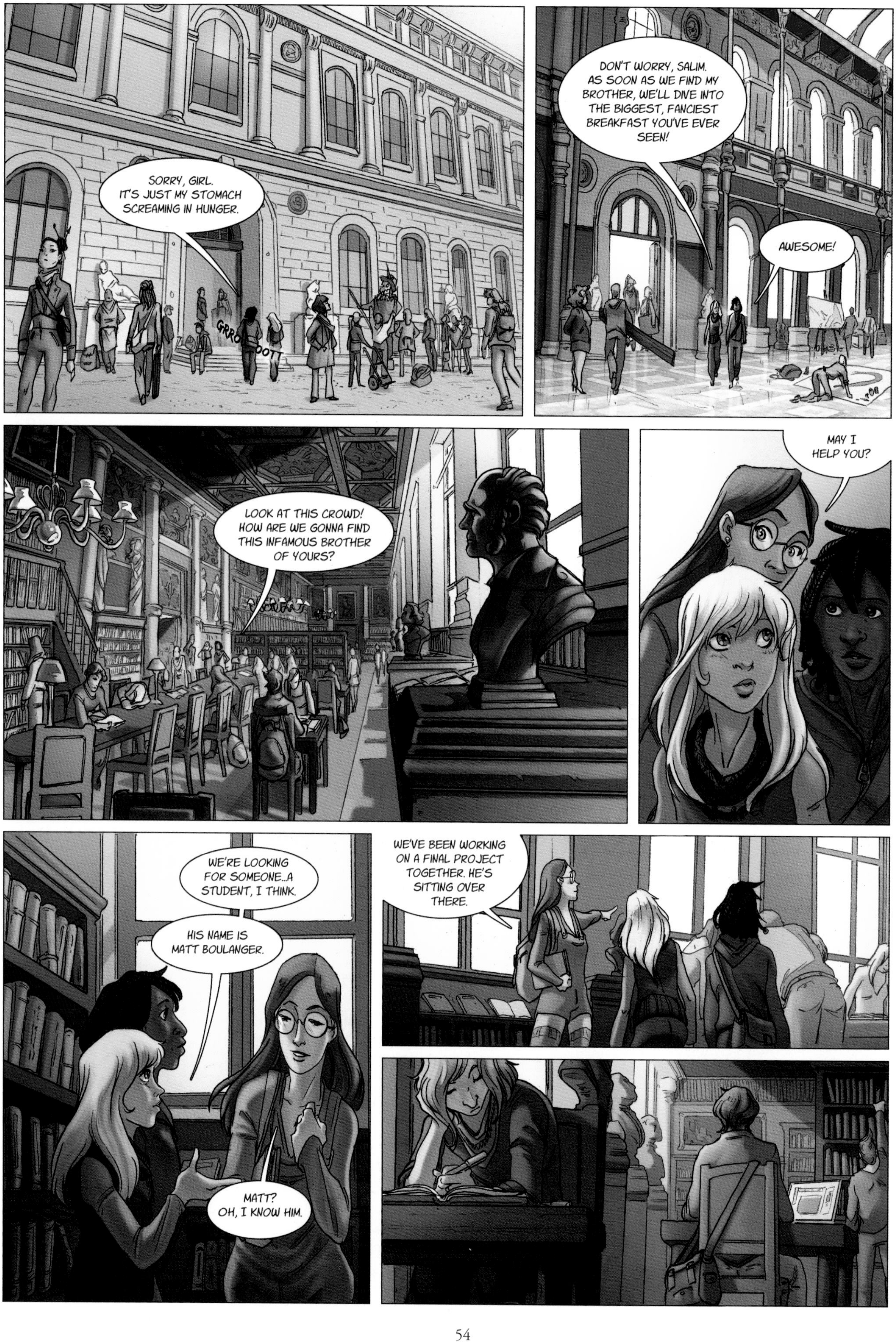
SORRY, GIRL.
IT'S JUST MY STOMACH SCREAMING IN HUNGER.
GRROOOOTT
DON'T WORRY, SALIM. AS SOON AS WE FIND MY BROTHER, WE'LL DIVE INTO THE BIGGEST, FANCIEST BREAKFAST YOU'VE EVER SEEN!
AWESOME!
LOOK AT THIS CROWD! HOW ARE WE GONNA FIND THIS INFAMOUS BROTHER OF YOURS?
MAY I HELP YOU?
WE'RE LOOKING FOR SOMEONE...A STUDENT, I THINK.
HIS NAME IS MATT BOULANGER.
MATT? OH, I KNOW HIM.
WE'VE BEEN WORKING ON A FINAL PROJECT TOGETHER. HE'S SITTING OVER THERE.

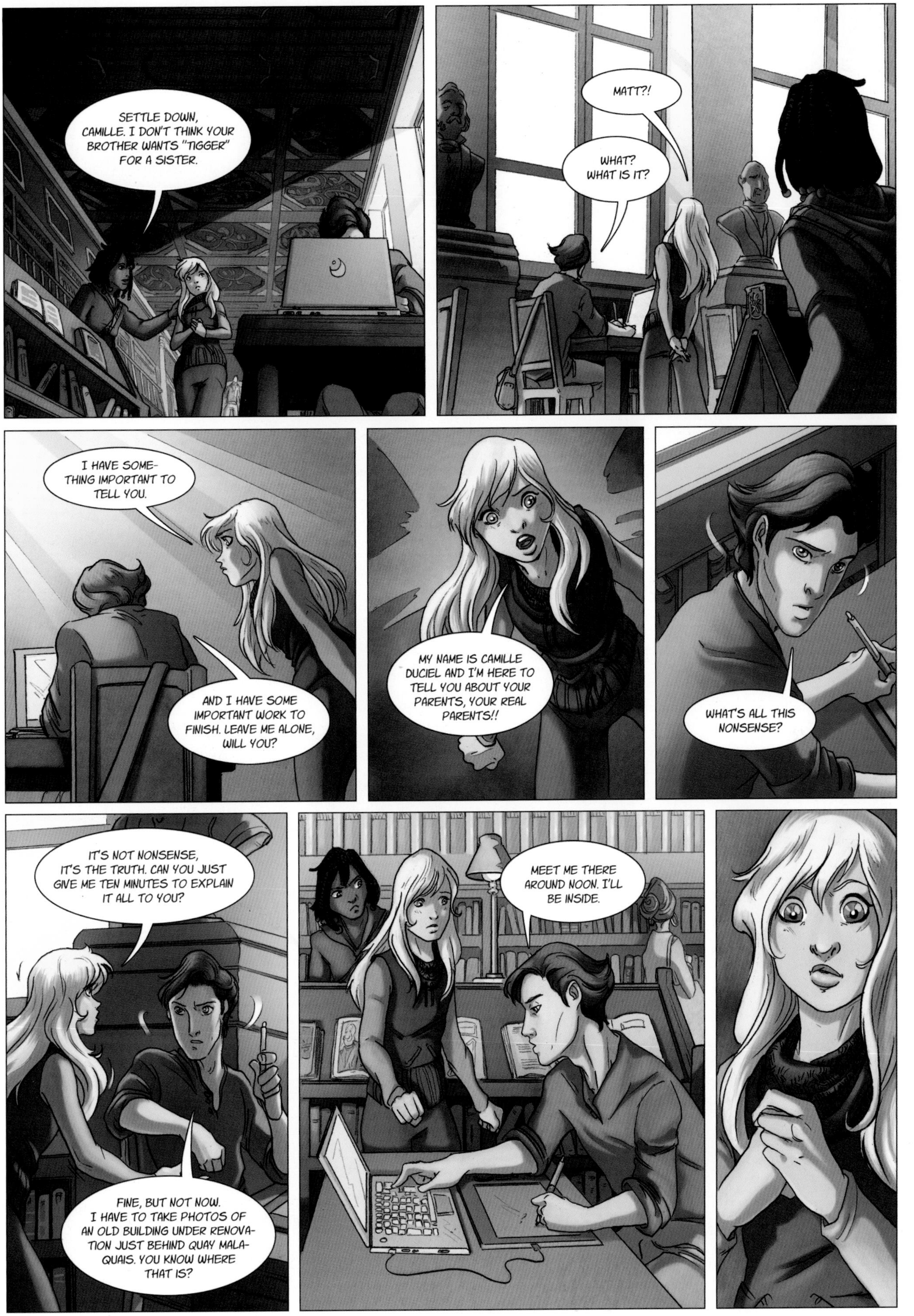
SETTLE DOWN, CAMILLE. I DON'T THINK YOUR BROTHER WANTS "TIGGER" FOR A SISTER.
MATT?!
WHAT? WHAT IS IT?
I HAVE SOME-THING IMPORTANT TO TELL YOU.
AND I HAVE SOME IMPORTANT WORK TO FINISH. LEAVE ME ALONE, WILL YOU?
MY NAME IS CAMILLE DUCIEL AND I'M HERE TO TELL YOU ABOUT YOUR PARENTS, YOUR REAL PARENTS!!
WHAT'S ALL THIS NONSENSE?
IT'S NOT NONSENSE, IT'S THE TRUTH. CAN YOU JUST GIVE ME TEN MINUTES TO EXPLAIN IT ALL TO YOU?
FINE, BUT NOT NOW. I HAVE TO TAKE PHOTOS OF AN OLD BUILDING UNDER RENOVA-TION JUST BEHIND QUAY MALA-QUAIS. YOU KNOW WHERE THAT IS?
MEET ME THERE AROUND NOON. I'LL BE INSIDE.

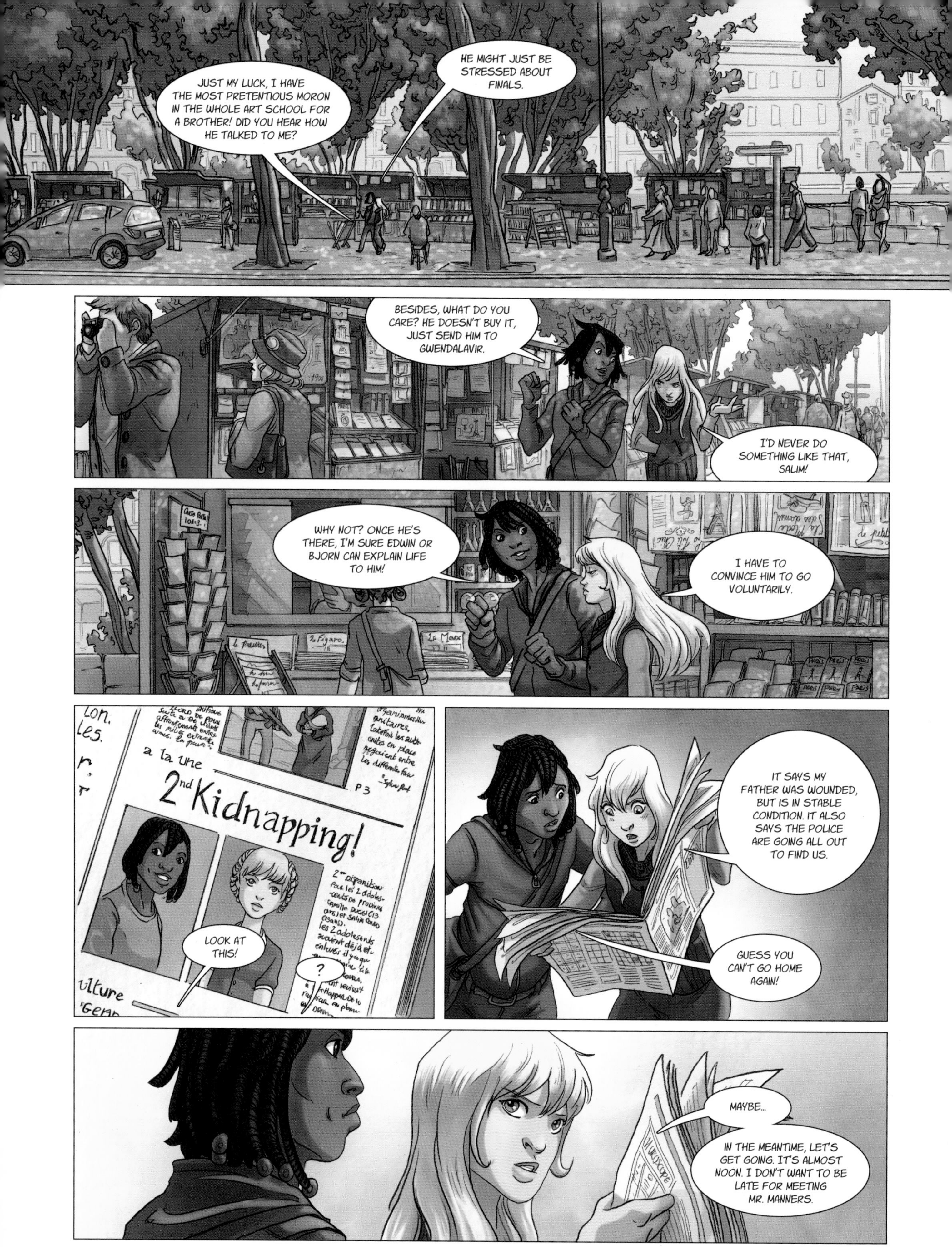
JUST MY LUCK, I HAVE THE MOST PRETENTIOUS MORON IN THE WHOLE ART SCHOOL FOR A BROTHER! DID YOU HEAR HOW HE TALKED TO ME?
HE MIGHT JUST BE STRESSED ABOUT FINALS.
BESIDES, WHAT DO YOU CARE? HE DOESN'T BUY IT, JUST SEND HIM TO GWENDALAVIR.
I'D NEVER DO SOMETHING LIKE THAT, SALIM!
WHY NOT? ONCE HE'S THERE, I'M SURE EDWIN OR BJORN CAN EXPLAIN LIFE TO HIM!
I HAVE TO CONVINCE HIM TO GO VOLUNTARILY.
a la une
2nd Kidnapping!
LOOK AT THIS!
?
IT SAYS MY FATHER WAS WOUNDED, BUT IS IN STABLE CONDITION. IT ALSO SAYS THE POLICE ARE GOING ALL OUT TO FIND US.
GUESS YOU CAN'T GO HOME AGAIN!
MAYBE...
IN THE MEANTIME, LET'S GET GOING. IT'S ALMOST NOON. I DON'T WANT TO BE LATE FOR MEETING MR. MANNERS.

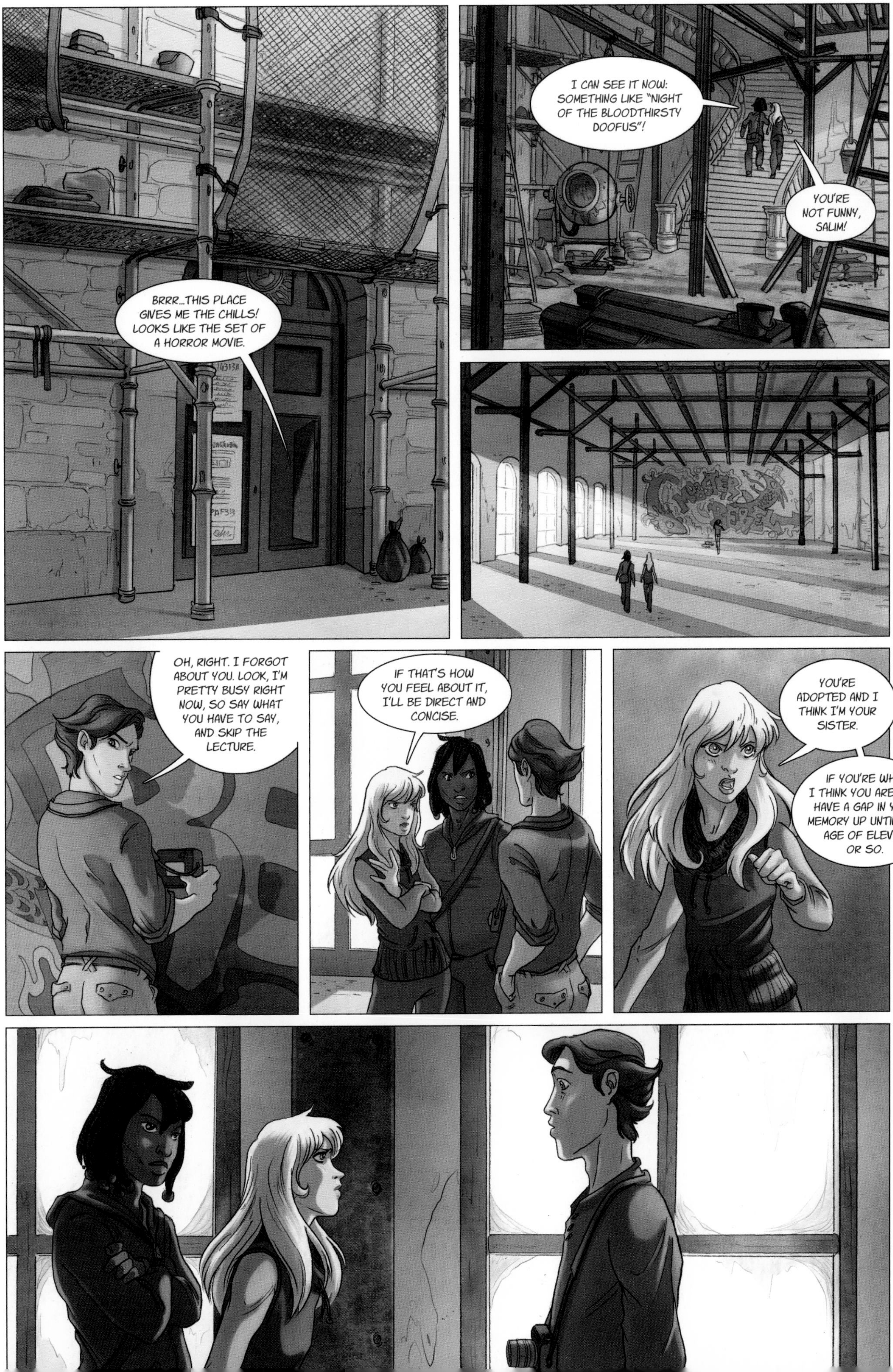
BRRR...THIS PLACE GIVES ME THE CHILLS! LOOKS LIKE THE SET OF A HORROR MOVIE.
I CAN SEE IT NOW: SOMETHING LIKE "NIGHT OF THE BLOODTHIRSTY DOOFUS"!
YOU'RE NOT FUNNY, SALIM!
OH, RIGHT. I FORGOT ABOUT YOU. LOOK, I'M PRETTY BUSY RIGHT NOW, SO SAY WHAT YOU HAVE TO SAY, AND SKIP THE LECTURE.
IF THAT'S HOW YOU FEEL ABOUT IT, I'LL BE DIRECT AND CONCISE.
YOU'RE ADOPTED AND I THINK I'M YOUR SISTER.
IF YOU'RE WHO I THINK YOU ARE, YOU HAVE A GAP IN YOUR MEMORY UP UNTIL THE AGE OF ELEVEN OR SO.

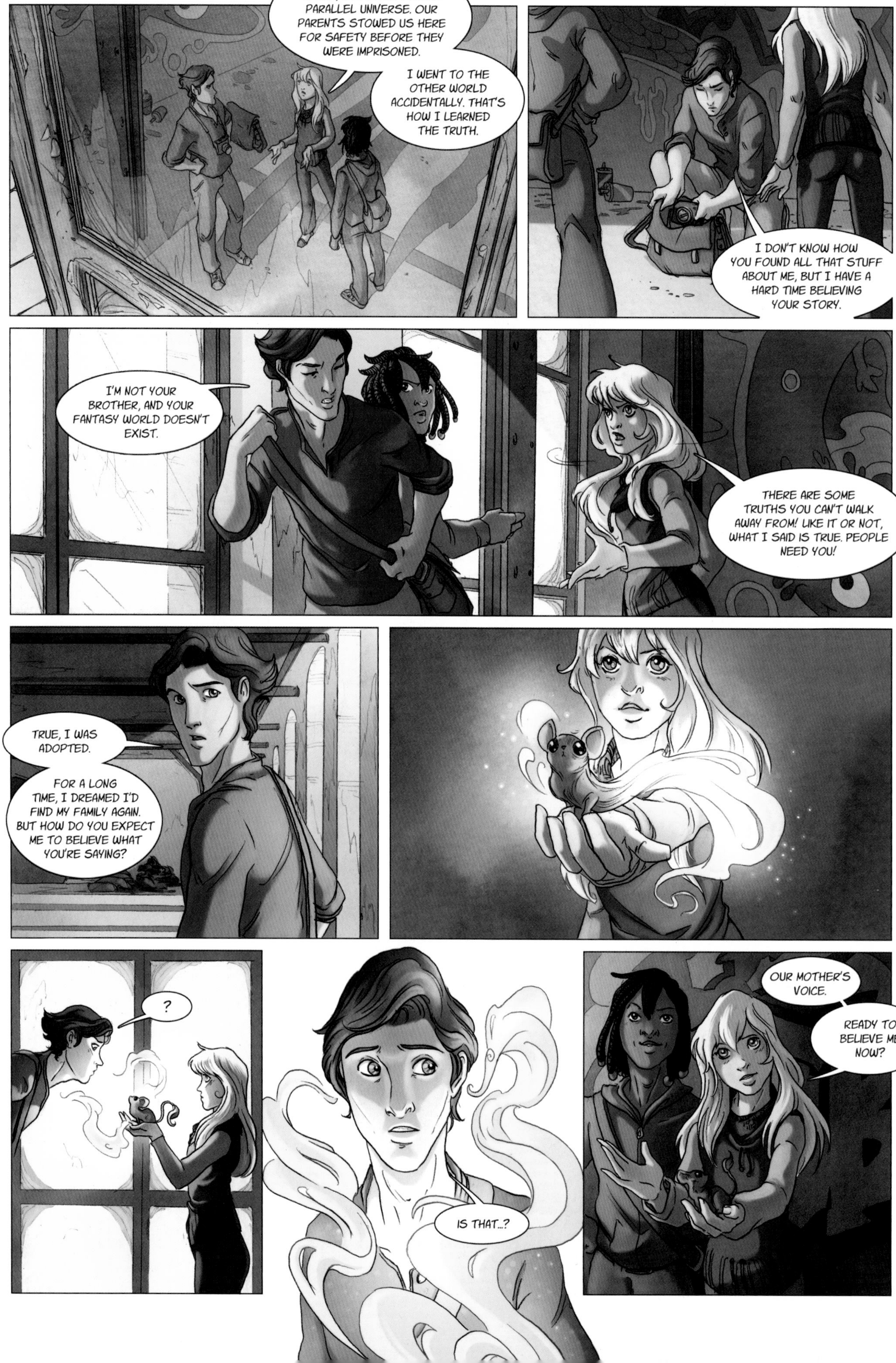
I KNOW IT SOUNDS WEIRD, BUT WE'RE FROM A PARALLEL UNIVERSE. OUR PARENTS STOWED US HERE FOR SAFETY BEFORE THEY WERE IMPRISONED.
I WENT TO THE OTHER WORLD ACCIDENTALLY. THAT'S HOW I LEARNED THE TRUTH.
I DON'T KNOW HOW YOU FOUND ALL THAT STUFF ABOUT ME, BUT I HAVE A HARD TIME BELIEVING YOUR STORY.
I'M NOT YOUR BROTHER, AND YOUR FANTASY WORLD DOESN'T EXIST.
THERE ARE SOME TRUTHS YOU CAN'T WALK AWAY FROM! LIKE IT OR NOT, WHAT I SAID IS TRUE. PEOPLE NEED YOU!
TRUE, I WAS ADOPTED.
FOR A LONG TIME, I DREAMED I'D FIND MY FAMILY AGAIN. BUT HOW DO YOU EXPECT ME TO BELIEVE WHAT YOU'RE SAYING?
?
IS THAT...?
OUR MOTHER'S VOICE.
READY TO BELIEVE ME NOW?

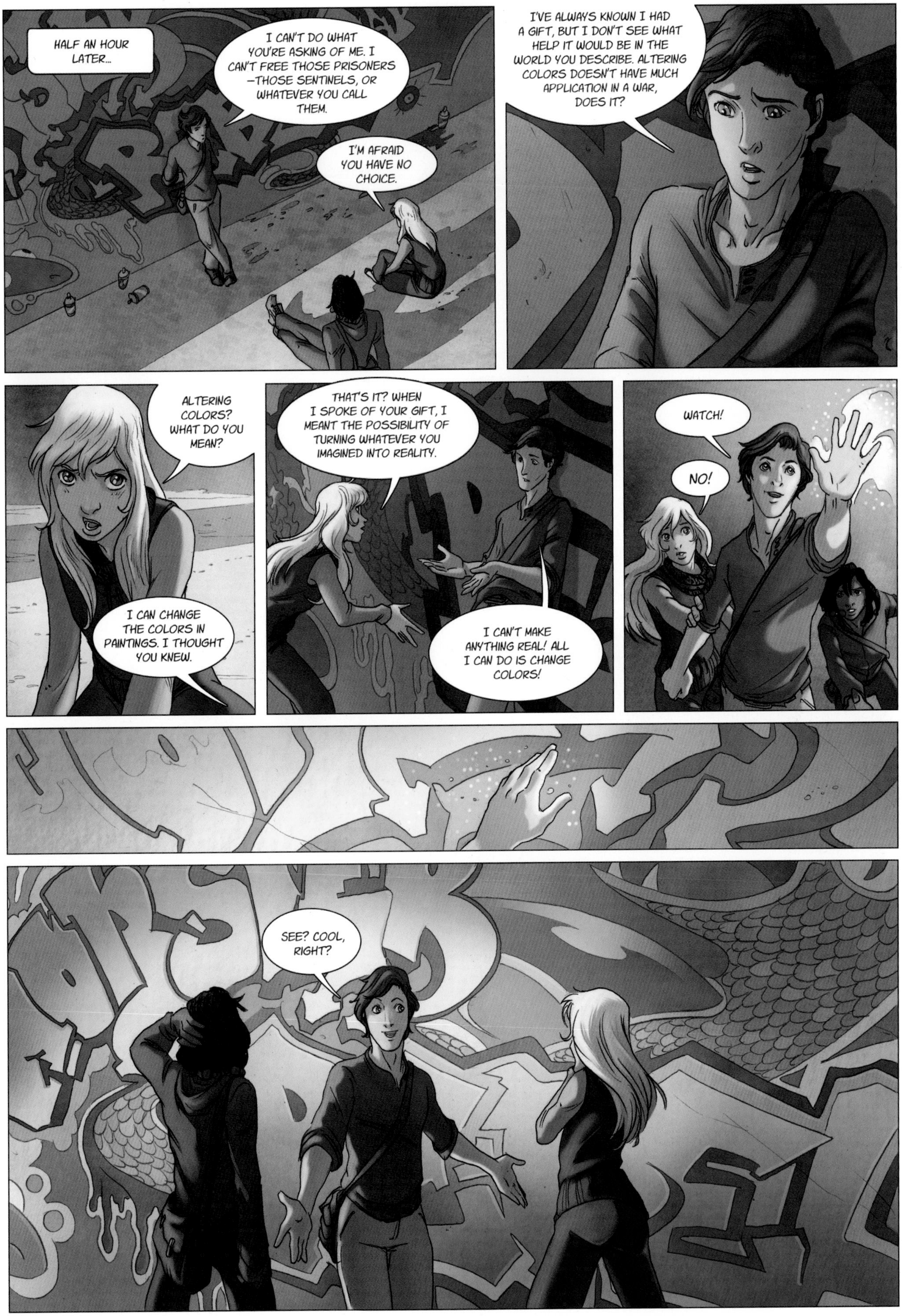
HALF AN HOUR LATER...
I CAN'T DO WHAT YOU'RE ASKING OF ME. I CAN'T FREE THOSE PRISONERS —THOSE SENTINELS, OR WHATEVER YOU CALL THEM.
I'M AFRAID YOU HAVE NO CHOICE.
I'VE ALWAYS KNOWN I HAD A GIFT, BUT I DON'T SEE WHAT HELP IT WOULD BE IN THE WORLD YOU DESCRIBE. ALTERING COLORS DOESN'T HAVE MUCH APPLICATION IN A WAR, DOES IT?
ALTERING COLORS? WHAT DO YOU MEAN?
I CAN CHANGE THE COLORS IN PAINTINGS. I THOUGHT YOU KNEW.
THAT'S IT? WHEN I SPOKE OF YOUR GIFT, I MEANT THE POSSIBILITY OF TURNING WHATEVER YOU IMAGINED INTO REALITY.
I CAN'T MAKE ANYTHING REAL! ALL I CAN DO IS CHANGE COLORS!
WATCH!
NO!
SEE? COOL, RIGHT?

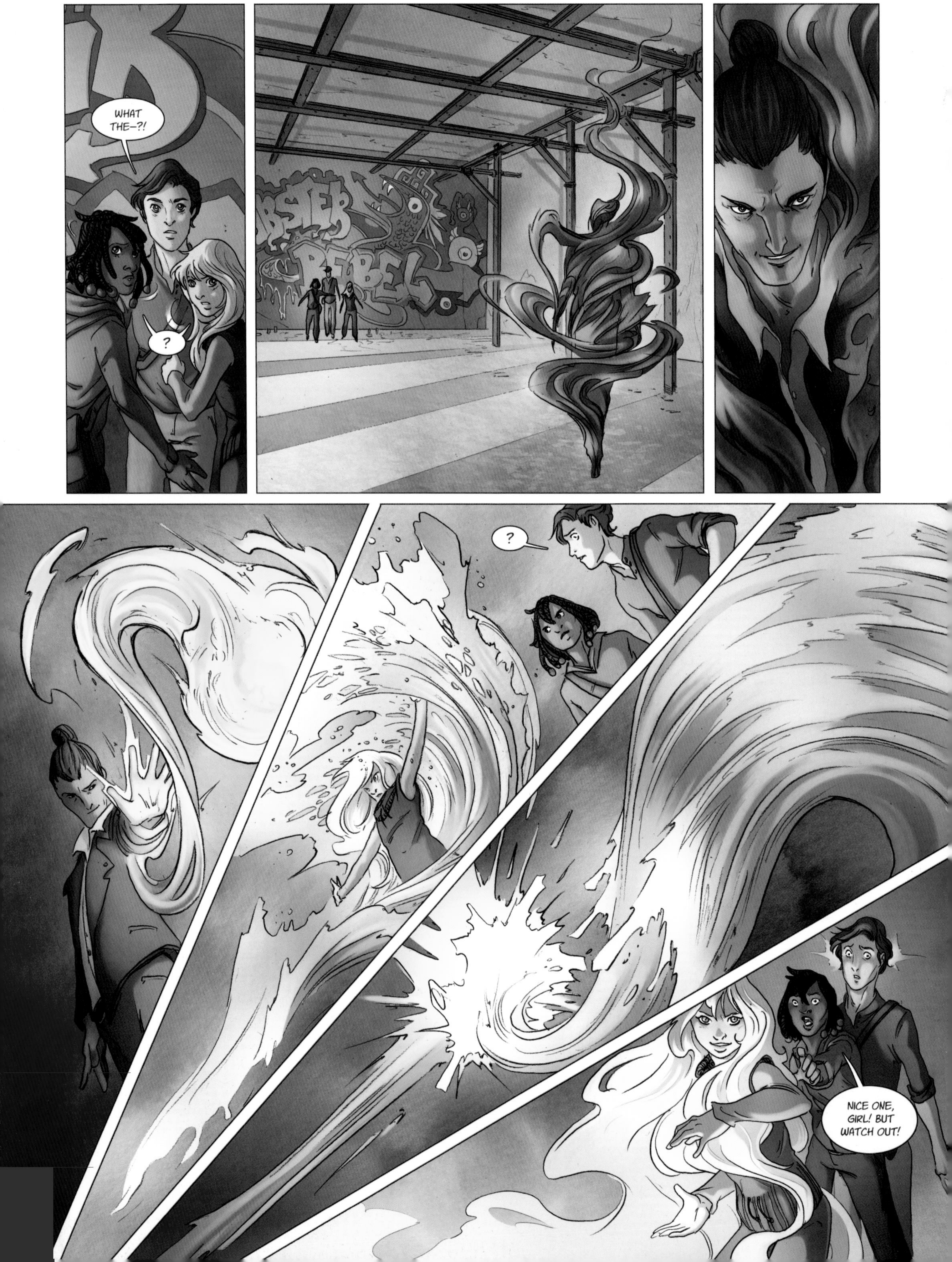
WHAT THE–?!
?
?
NICE ONE, GIRL! BUT WATCH OUT!

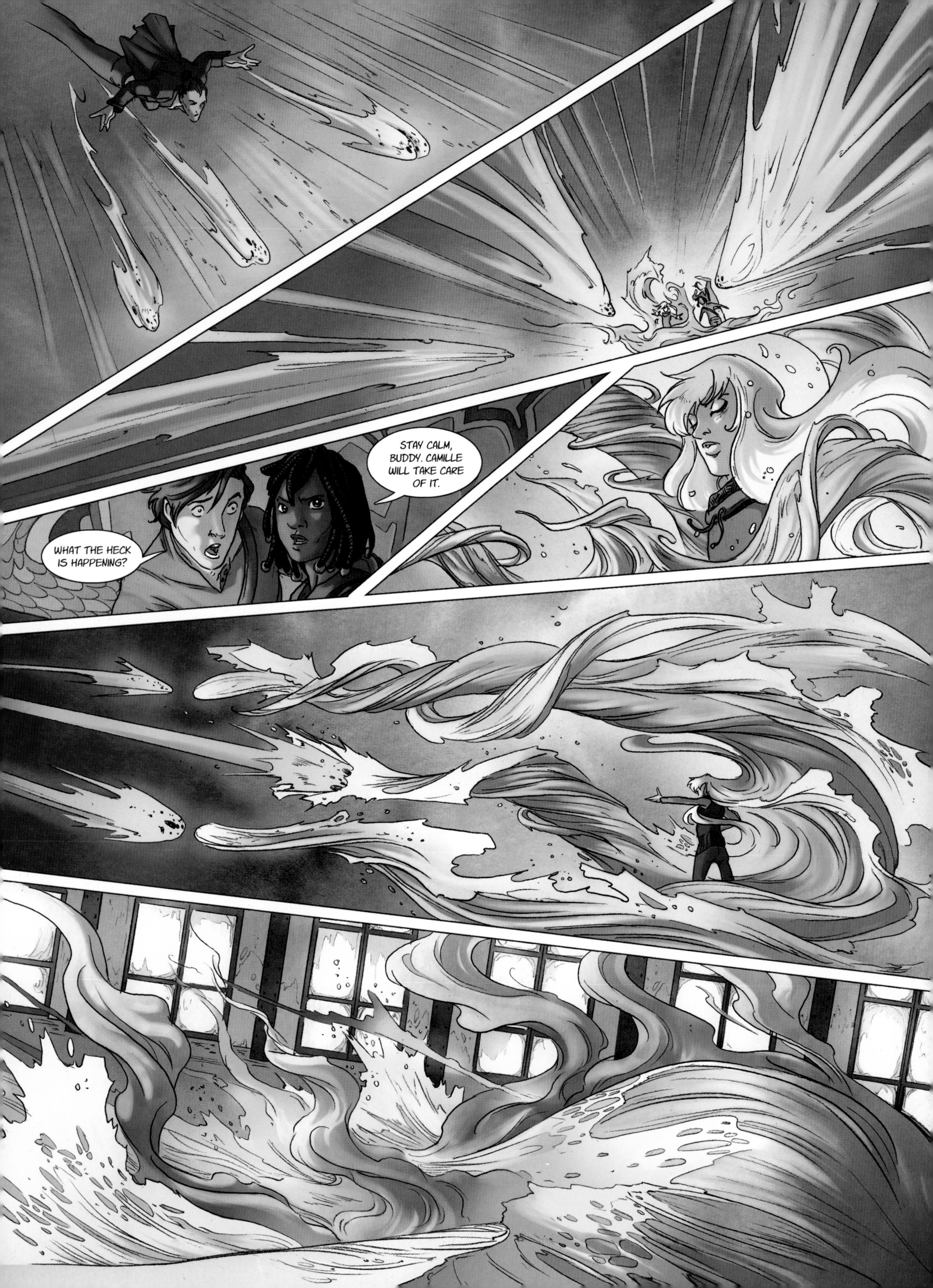
WHAT THE HECK IS HAPPENING?
STAY CALM, BUDDY. CAMILLE WILL TAKE CARE OF IT.

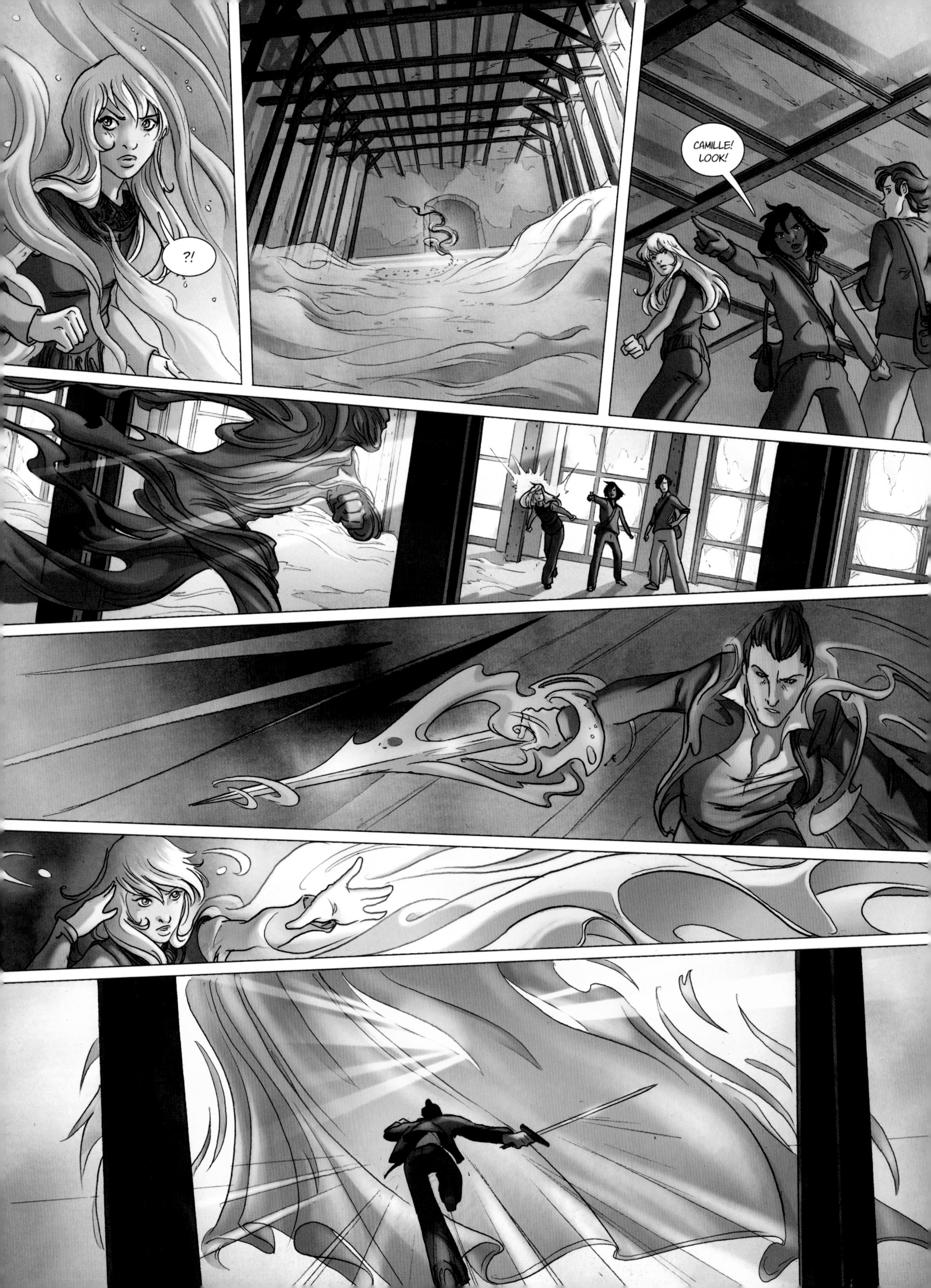
?!
CAMILLE! LOOK!

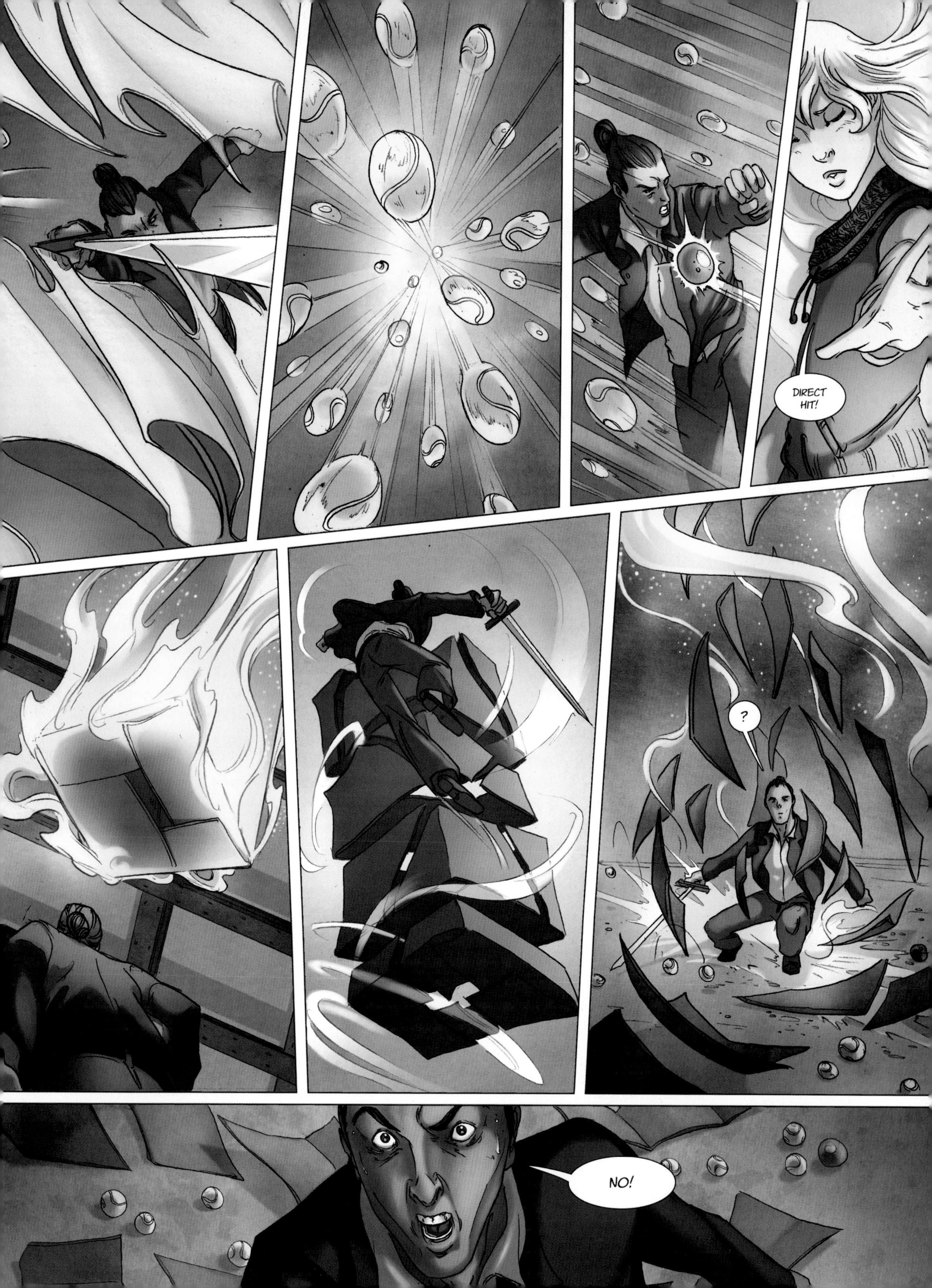
DIRECT HIT!
?
NO!

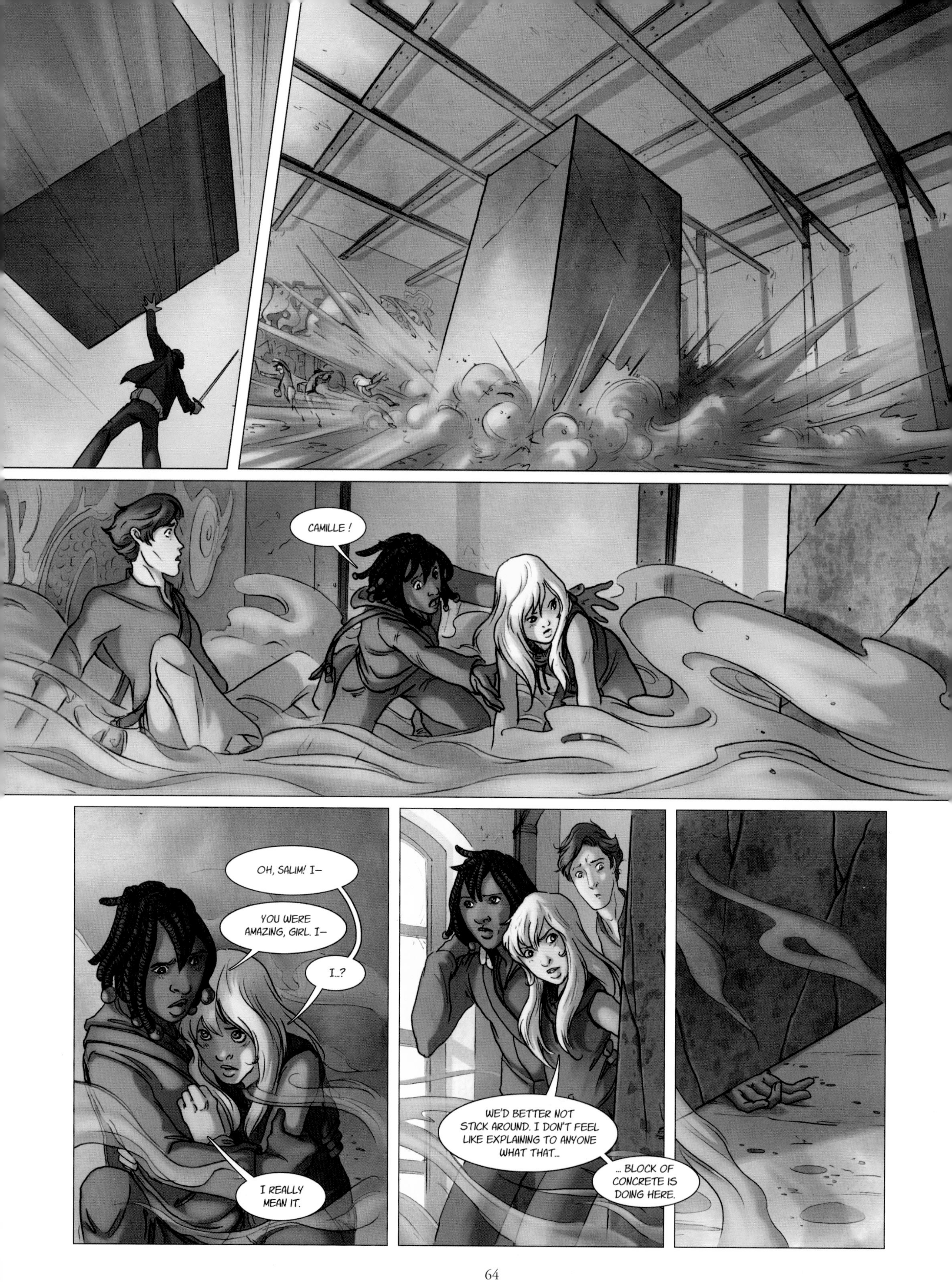
CAMILLE !
OH, SALIM! I–
YOU WERE AMAZING, GIRL. I–
I...?
I REALLY MEAN IT.
WE'D BETTER NOT STICK AROUND. I DON'T FEEL LIKE EXPLAINING TO ANYONE WHAT THAT...
... BLOCK OF CONCRETE IS DOING HERE.

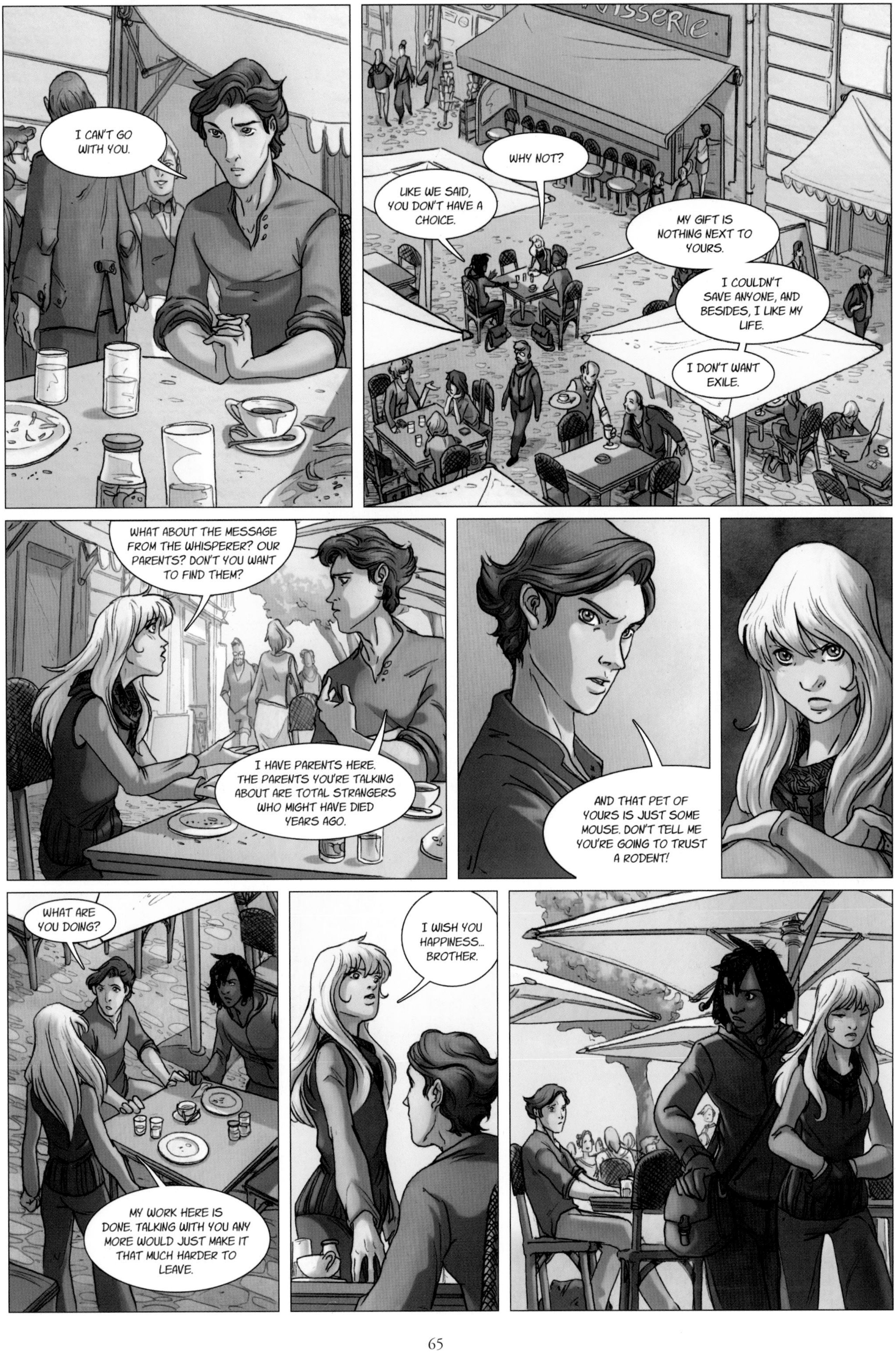
I CAN'T GO WITH YOU.
WHY NOT?
LIKE WE SAID, YOU DON'T HAVE A CHOICE.
MY GIFT IS NOTHING NEXT TO YOURS.
I COULDN'T SAVE ANYONE, AND BESIDES, I LIKE MY LIFE.
I DON'T WANT EXILE.
WHAT ABOUT THE MESSAGE FROM THE WHISPERER? OUR PARENTS? DON'T YOU WANT TO FIND THEM?
I HAVE PARENTS HERE. THE PARENTS YOU'RE TALKING ABOUT ARE TOTAL STRANGERS WHO MIGHT HAVE DIED YEARS AGO.
AND THAT PET OF YOURS IS JUST SOME MOUSE. DON'T TELL ME YOU'RE GOING TO TRUST A RODENT!
WHAT ARE YOU DOING?
MY WORK HERE IS DONE. TALKING WITH YOU ANY MORE WOULD JUST MAKE IT THAT MUCH HARDER TO LEAVE.
I WISH YOU HAPPINESS... BROTHER.

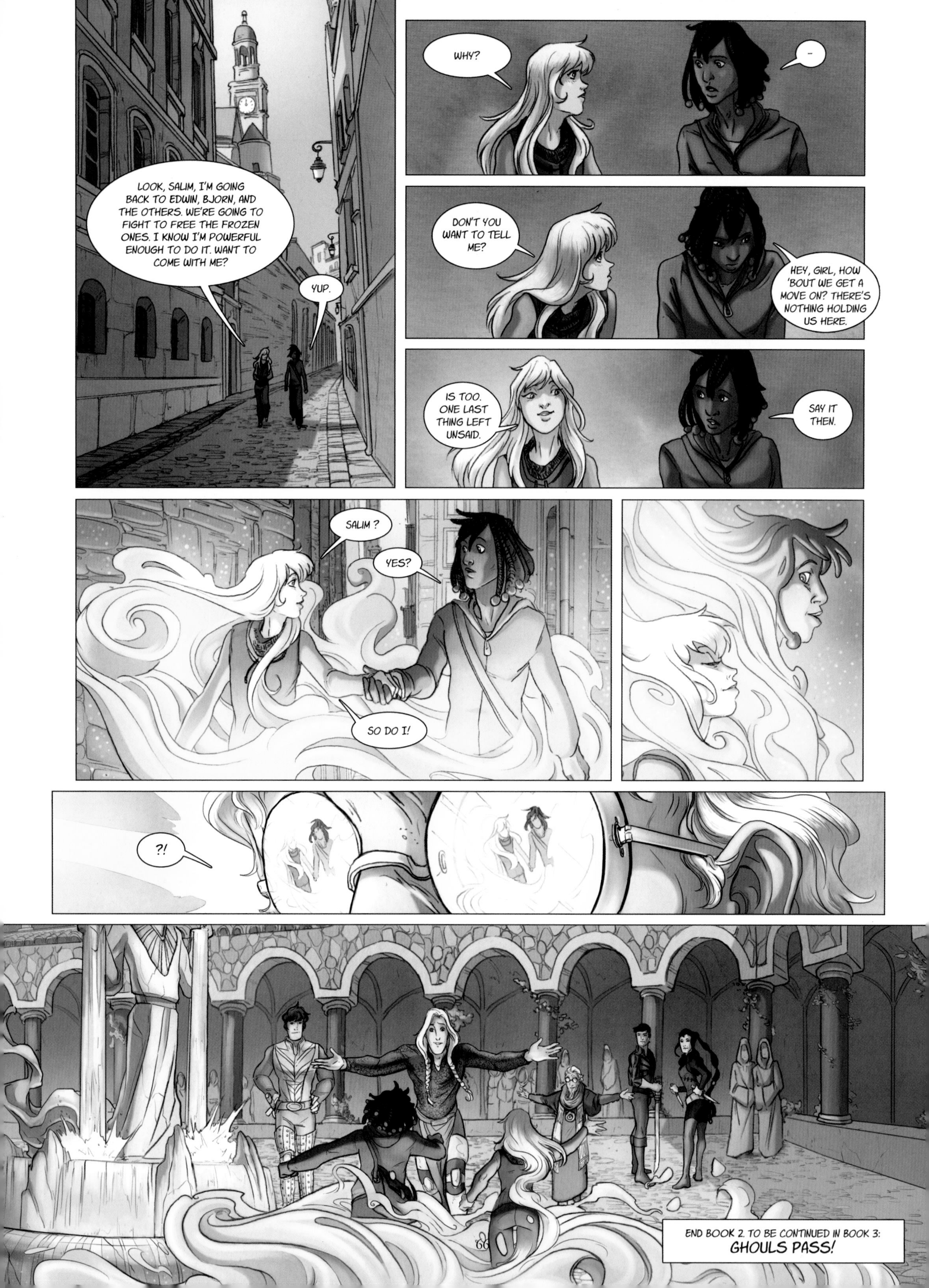
LOOK, SALIM, I'M GOING BACK TO EDWIN, BJORN, AND THE OTHERS. WE'RE GOING TO FIGHT TO FREE THE FROZEN ONES. I KNOW I'M POWERFUL ENOUGH TO DO IT. WANT TO COME WITH ME?
YUP.
WHY?
...
DON'T YOU WANT TO TELL ME?
HEY, GIRL, HOW 'BOUT WE GET A MOVE ON? THERE'S NOTHING HOLDING US HERE.
IS TOO. ONE LAST THING LEFT UNSAID.
SAY IT THEN.
SALIM ?
YES?
SO DO I!
?!
END BOOK 2. TO BE CONTINUED IN BOOK 3:
GHOULS PASS!

OTHER BOOKS FROM EuroComics/IDW

Corto Maltese by Hugo Pratt

The Adventures of Dieter Lumpen
by Jorge Zentner & Rubén Pellejero

The Silence of Malka
by Jorge Zentner & Rubén Pellejero

Paracuellos by Carlos Giménez

Flight of the Raven by Jean-Pierre Gibrat

The Reprieve by Jean-Pierre Gibrat

Mattéo by Jean-Pierre Gibrat

Alack Sinner by Carlos Sampayo & José Muñoz

Jerome K. Jerome Bloche by Alain Dodier

Lights of the Amalou
by Christophe Gibelin & Claire Wendling

**One Man, One Adventure:
The Man from the Great North**
by Hugo Pratt

Tales from the Age of the Cobra
by Enrique Fernández

Violette
by Teresa Radice & Stefano Turconi

Four Sisters
by Malika Ferdjoukh & Cati Baur

Enola Holmes
by Serena Blasco and Nancy Springer

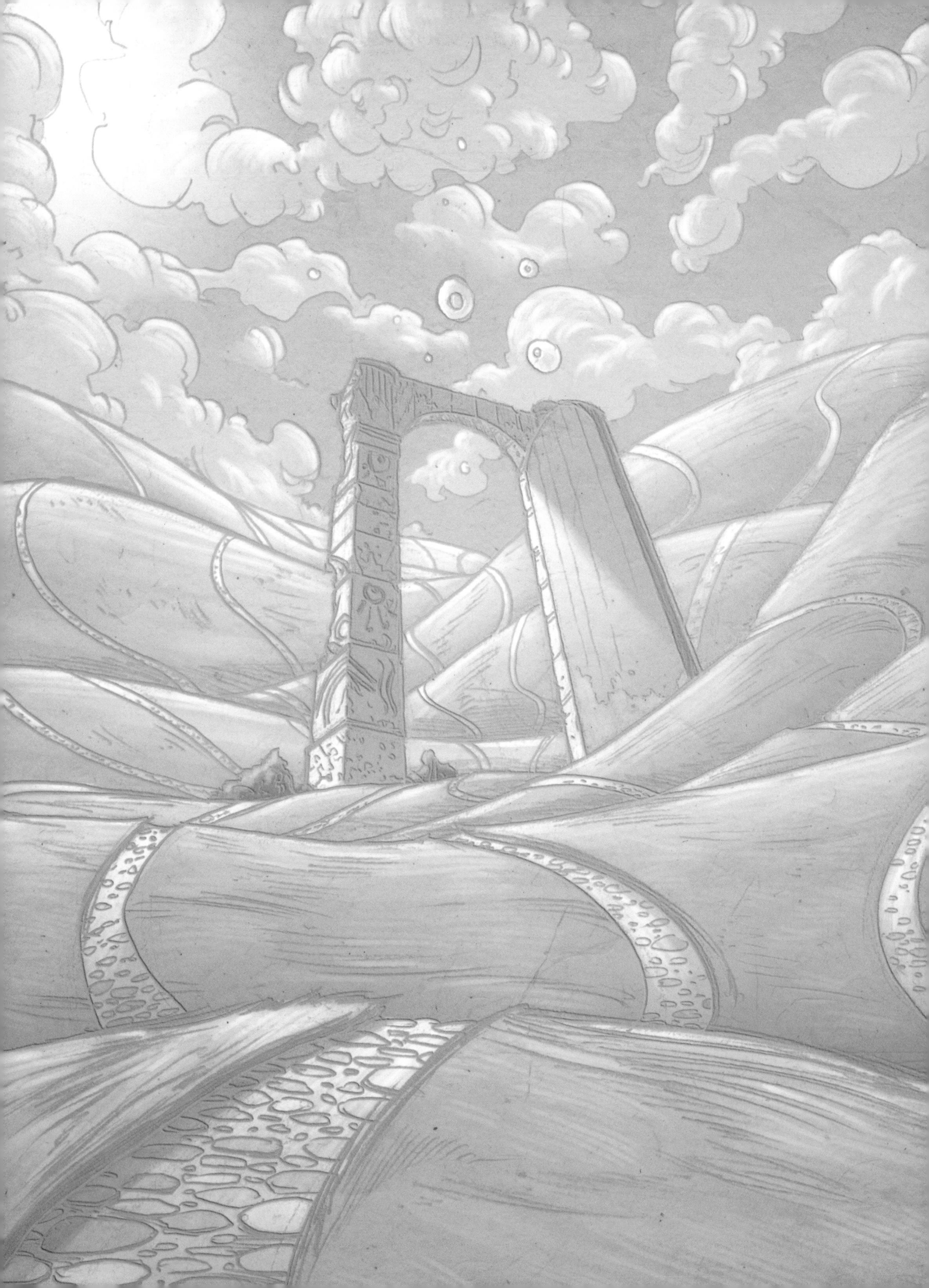